D1525475

THE LADY'S SECOND-CHANCE SUITOR
Grace by the Sea, Book 5

Copyright © 2021 by Regina Lundgren

All rights reserved. Except for use in any review, the reproduction or utilization of this work in whole or in part in any form by any electronic, mechanical or other means, now known or hereinafter invented, including xerography, photocopying and recording, or in any information storage or retrieval system, is forbidden without the written permission of the publisher.

This is a work of fiction. Names, characters, places and incidents are either the product of the author's imagination or are used fictitiously, and any resemblance to actual persons, living or dead, business establishments, events or locales is entirely coincidental.

Printed in the USA.

Cover Design and Interior Format

GRACE
-BY-THE-
SEA
5

The Lady's Second-Chance Suitor

REGINA SCOTT

To the readers and authors who make Lady Catherine's Salon on Facebook such a warm, welcoming community—thank you for generously sharing your love of Regency romances! And to the Lord, who welcomes us all to His community.

CHAPTER ONE

Grace-by-the-Sea, Dorset, England, September 1804

WHY DID SHE COMPARE EVERY man to him? Hester Todd smiled up at the silver-haired baron who had requested her hand in the dance. Lord Feather-stone was a Regular at Grace-by-the-Sea, meaning that he could be found daily at the spa that supported the village, and he was a well-known figure among the shops and at assemblies like this one. He was old enough to be her father and then some, though he danced with the elegance and grace that fellows half his age might envy. He was well dressed, well spoken, a gentleman in all ways.

But he would never be as dashing as Rob Peverell. She felt no spark of excitement when his gaze brushed hers, no giddy anticipation that their fingers might meet.

She'd learned there was something to be said for a lack of giddy anticipation. Peace and stability were not unwel-come, particularly as she had her daughter, Rebecca, to think of now.

Of course, peace was at a premium at the moment. The Harvest Ball was one of the most crowded of the year. Anyone from kitchen maid to lord of the manor might attend. The lovely pale blue walls of the assembly rooms were all but invisible behind the throngs of attendees. Muslin and cotton skirts swept past those of silk and fine wool. Rough-spun coats bumped shoulders against tai-lored velvet. It was a wonder the candles in the crystal chandelier didn't start melting from the rising warmth alone.

The music stopped; the dance ended. She curtsied to Lord Featherstone's bow, and he offered her his arm to escort her back to the wall, where the other widows awaited similar kindnesses.

"You are an accomplished dancer, Mrs. Todd," he said. "I appreciate you honoring my request, particularly when you have so deservedly attracted such a train of followers."

She and Rosemary, her sister, had garnered their fair share of late. Newcomers at the spa, such as the dapper Mr. Donner, who had been her first partner of the eve-ning; curly-haired, curious Mr. Cushman; shy Mr. Nash; and determined Mr. Fenton; as well as an officer or two from the camp at West Creech and Alex Chance, younger brother of their sister-in-law, Jesslyn, the spa hostess. It ought to be gratifying.

Why did she persist in seeking a dusky blond, tousle-haired head among them?

"You are too kind, my lord," she told Lord Feather-stone. "I would be delighted to dance with you whenever you have a free moment. But you too have amassed quite a following." She nodded to where Lady Howland was gazing in their direction. It was not quite a glare—the widowed countess was far too polished for that—but the look was decidedly chilly. It seemed the lady thought the gentleman hers.

He, apparently, did not. "No one who could eclipse my affections for you," he said with a gallant bow to Hester. "I envy the gentlemen who will beg for your hand in the next dances."

She inclined her head, and he strolled off, away from the countess, who huffed and stalked in the opposite direction. Well, at least Hester wasn't the only lady who made a favored gentleman run.

She took a seat on one of the few open chairs, trying to shake the feelings that crowded her more surely than the other attendees. It had been seven years since she'd laid eyes on Rob. If she thought of anyone with longing, it should be Lieutenant Jasper Todd, her late husband, father to her daughter.

She drew in a breath and glanced around the room, only to spy Rosemary strolling away from the dancefloor on the arm of her employer, the Earl of Howland. How proud Rosemary had been to win the position of governess to the earl's daughter. But Hester had seen more in the way the handsome widower gazed at her sister.

Rosemary was brave and clever. She'd worked with their uncle to learn all manner of things, including how to scurry about the cliffsides searching for evidence of ancient life. She was a devoted sister, a loving aunt to Hester's daughter. There wasn't much Hester wouldn't do for Rosemary, even to taking the earl aside for a private word.

"What!" Her darker-haired sister had yelped when she'd heard of it at one of the weekly assemblies in this very room. "What did you say to him?"

"I asked him his intentions," Hester admitted, "and warned him about sullying your reputation."

Rosemary snorted. "I'm surprised he didn't sack me immediately. What were you thinking?"

"I was thinking of you," Hester informed her. "An earl taking interest in a commoner? You know where that could lead."

"He is no Rob Peverell," Rosemary insisted. "I've not heard any stories of dalliances or flirting. He was by all accounts a devoted husband and remains a loving father."

Hester regarded her sadly. "Yes, I will grant you others claim him beyond reproach. But you are still in his employ, and he is an earl. It isn't seemly."

Rosemary sagged, as if all the fire had gone out of her. "I know. I could tell you it is all in your imagination, but he sent me flowers yesterday."

Which only proved how little Lord Howland understood the tragedies she and her bluestocking sister had survived. Hester touched her arm. "I'm so sorry. He couldn't know."

"Of course he couldn't know. I explained myself a few moments ago, so it shouldn't happen again."

She should hope not. She hadn't the aversion to the blossoms her sister had, but she would never forget finding their father dead among the wildflowers. He had been attacked by the smugglers he had sought to apprehend as a Riding Officer for the Excise Office. She and Rosemary had relied on each other then, while their mother and older brother dealt with moving the family from Kent to Upper Grace to live with their mother's brother. The only thing that had ever threatened to drive her and Rosemary apart had been Rob Peverell.

She raised her head now. Enough of these thoughts! She must find her next dance partner. She stood and set off around the edge of the dancefloor, as if she were intent on some errand. Still, memories chased her.

Rob, racing her down the road on horseback.

Rob, laughing as he spun her in a circle among the waving grass of the Downs.

Rob, meeting her on the shore to watch the sun set in a glory that was as fiery as his kiss.

Rob, disappearing with only the most casual of farewells, leaving her hurting.

No, no! She had made a fool of herself over a handsome stranger who had turned out to be the younger son of Viscount Peverell, one of the two local landowners. It had been humiliating, heart-breaking. But good had come of it. Because of her wounded heart, she had carefully considered Jasper's proposal of marriage when he'd been home between assignments in the Navy. Because she'd married her lieutenant, she now had a beautiful six-year-old daughter who brightened her life. Because of Rebecca's birth, her mother had opened her home to them, so Hester always had somewhere safe to live. Because she'd been widowed, she'd been accepted as the teacher for the dame school in Upper Grace, helping young minds to grow. And because of her service, she could live with her head high, a pillar of the community, respected wherever she went. Truly, it was all a blessing.

"Excuse me, dearie." A farmwife shoved past on her way to the door. Hester stepped back to avoid her and collided with a solid frame.

She turned to apologize, and the words dried up in her mouth.

Rob Peverell stared at her, light hazel eyes darkened by his evening black, hair tousled, chin just beginning to hint of stubble.

"Gwen?" he asked.

She wanted to shoot into the sky like one of Mr. Congreve's rockets, explode in a flash of lightning, sink to the bottom of the cove. Her cheeks were hot, her muscles frozen. Somehow, she managed to find her voice.

"You are mistaken, sir. I do not know you."

Then she turned and fled as fast as dignity allowed.

"Who was that?" his sister asked.

Rob, the recently elevated Viscount Peverell, shook his head. "I thought I knew, but perhaps she's right. Perhaps I was mistaken."

Elizabeth's hazel gaze, so like his own, followed the honey-haired beauty as she hurried away from them, ruby-colored silk skirts swaying. "She certainly didn't care for you. That was nearly the cut direct."

It had been. Over the years, he'd deserved it on any number of occasions. His dalliance with Guinevere Ascot had been one of them. Yet surely someone so lovely, so warm and giving as Gwen would have been long married. It had been, what, seven years now? She would have changed.

He was doing his best to change.

"Lord Peverell, Miss Peverell." The pretty hostess of the spa smiled at them as she approached, the curls at the sides of her face glinting like gold. "I've been asked to introduce you to several of our Regulars. Would that be permissible?"

Mrs. Denby had been a dewy-eyed miss, helping her hostess mother and physician father at the spa, when last he'd visited the area. His father and brother had been alive then, and he'd let them carry most of the conversations on the rare occasion they consented to appear in the village. He'd needed more than the spa, the village shops, and the assembly to enliven him.

Gwen had been everything he had wanted and more.

Now he inclined his head. "We'd be delighted. Perhaps first, you could answer a question for me. Do you know Miss Guinevere Ascot?"

She tapped her chin with one finger. "I don't believe we've ever had a guest by that name, and certainly no one locally."

He nodded across the room, to where a young military officer in scarlet regimentals was escorting Gwen out onto the floor. "What about that lady?"

She followed his gaze, and her smile warmed. "My sister-in-law, Mrs. Todd. But her first name isn't Guinevere. It's Hester."

"And her husband?" Elizabeth put in with a glance to Rob. "A stalwart sort, protective of his lady, perhaps?"

Did she think he intended to carry Hester Todd off? Once, perhaps, but not now. Too much depended on him finding a way to pretend he knew how to be the viscount.

"He was a valiant lieutenant in the Navy," Mrs. Denby assured his sister. "Gone now these past six years. Mrs. Todd teaches at the dame school in Upper Grace. Did you wish an introduction, my lord?"

Elizabeth narrowed her eyes at him.

"No, thank you," Rob made himself say. "But we will await your good pleasure on the others."

She nodded and swept off to find those desirous of making his acquaintance. Mrs. Todd would not be among them.

He couldn't have mistaken her. She had to be his Gwen.

She'd been rather proud of that name. "Guinevere," she'd said with a toss of her silky mane when he'd asked the intimacy of using her first name. "Like Arthur's queen."

"Then you shall be mine," Rob had vowed.

If she had given him a false name instead of her own, it had been only his due. He certainly hadn't advertised his name. His father would have had apoplexy if he'd known his younger son was improving a boring summer by romancing a local lass.

Beside him, Elizabeth's feet shuffled below her lavender silk skirts. "After Mrs. Denby makes these introductions, may we go? I'm not as ready as I thought to rejoin Society. I'm finding this all a bit much."

It was. And it was exactly the sort of evening he normally enjoyed. Dozens of people from all walks of life, mixing, laughing, conversing, dancing. Constant movement, constant buzz. No fellow could be bored in such a place.

But he was the head of the family now. He must think of more than his own pleasure. The act was still foreign, but necessary.

"Of course," he promised.

A short time later, he skillfully extricated himself and Elizabeth from a scintillating conversation about the weather and left the crowded assembly rooms behind. His coach was waiting. They had only to step inside before they were swept along the headland to the west of the village. He peered out, thinking of how many times he'd raced along these roads, but the sight of his triumphs eluded him. In fact, the carriage lamps made it difficult to see more than his own reflection out the window. And he'd had entirely too much time to reflect on himself of late.

"So," Elizabeth said, crossing her arms over her chest as he turned to face her. "Who is she, Rob?"

He did not want to have this conversation. "The goggle-eyed Mrs. Greer who gushed all over you? I distinctly remember our charming hostess saying she is the wife of the Spa Corporation Council president, who is the village allegory? No, actuary?"

"Apothecary," Elizabeth reminded him with a small smile. "And you know very well I wasn't referring to her."

"Glad I am to hear it. I would not want to think you had fallen into the habit of encouraging a sycophant, unless it is me, of course. Though, if you have, I might bring to your attention that pimple-faced youth who kept staring at you."

"Rob." Her voice hinted of both reproach and laughter. "Who is Hester Todd to you?"

"Apparently someone who would prefer not to renew our acquaintance."

She lowered her arms. "And why? Is there some scandal involved? You said you would like us to stay here through the winter. If I am to associate with these people, I should know if there's a matter best left unspoken."

THE LADY'S SECOND-CHANCE SUITOR   15

"Precisely why I would prefer not to speak of it."

She rolled her eyes. "I will have the truth. You know that. You never could keep anything from me."

Far more than she realized, but Rob merely smiled at her. "Yes, you can be quite the sleuth when you put your mind to it."

She leaned forward. "And my mind is entirely engaged with thoughts of this Mrs. Todd. Where did you meet? What were you to each other? Are you intent on pursuing her now?"

Rob sighed. "Very well. You're right that someone else may know the tale, though we both tried hard to keep it quiet."

"Oooh," she said, leaning back, eyes kindling. "Secrets. Do tell."

"It is not to my credit, I assure you."

When she still regarded him, waiting, he knew there was nothing for it. "You may remember the summer you were finishing your first Season. Father, Thomas, and I came out to the Lodge to escape the London heat. They were quite content to while away the days reading, playing at draughts, and sailing. I wanted more."

She nodded. "Of course you did."

"Since I found the spa set insipid, I sought better game afield. Thinking to throw Father off the scent, I dressed like a commoner and took to strolling through Upper Grace until I fell in with a group of fellows about my age who knew how to have fun."

"Fun," she said, as if the word were foreign to her. "Racing horses, gambling, seducing women?"

"Certainly plenty of the first two, though not much of the last, I'm sorry to say."

She raised an eloquent brow.

"It's true," Rob insisted. "You will find the ladies of the area a clever lot. They were proof against even my considerable charms."

"How refreshing."

"I found it a challenge," Rob admitted, "and all the more so when we happened upon a young lady taking a walk out from the village. The others treated her with all deference and urged me to be off. I was instantly smitten and demanded to know more about her. She was reticent at first, but I soon won her over. She told me she was the daughter of a well-to-do merchant, who closely watched her comings and goings. She had barely managed to escape the house that day by climbing from her bedroom window."

"And that only made her more of a challenge," Elizabeth guessed.

"Of course. Nothing like a little subterfuge to whet the appetite."

"We can skip the part about your appetites," she informed him.

"No more than a few stolen kisses," he assured her. "She was in all ways the epitome of a lady in my eyes. She could do no wrong, and she felt the same about me. We spent part of nearly every day together."

She sighed, face softening in the lamplight. "How wildly romantic."

Was that envy in his little sister's voice?

"I thought so at the time," he said, "but I must caution you against attempting the feat. Someone always gets hurt."

Her face slumped. "Apparently Mrs. Todd."

"She must have been unmarried then," he said. "But yes, I have no doubt my defection hurt her. That is the saddest part of the tale. When Father was ready to return to London, I rather blithely told my angel that I would be leaving the area, but thank you very kindly for making my summer bearable. I doubt she knew who I truly was until then."

"Oh, Rob." She shook her head. "You're right. It is a

sad tale. You were reprehensible. At least you are trying to change."

The word *trying* stung, but he could not denounce the truth of it. He'd been born the coddled second son, with no expectations of greatness, no pressure to perform. He'd done what he'd liked, and money or charm had resolved most of the consequences.

One tragic afternoon on the Thames, one vessel with everyone aboard lost, had changed all that. Now his sister, his tenants, and their family fortune depended on him doing the right thing, every time. He might have removed himself from the whirl of London, but a dozen duties awaited him at the Lodge on the headland even now.

His father would have found him a sad trial, for the thoughts foremost in his mind were those of Hester Todd and how he could go about seeing her again.

CHAPTER TWO

HESTER FINISHED THE DANCE WITH Captain Cunningham from the encampment at West Creech and allowed him to lead her back to the wall. The dark-haired fellow looked as if he would have liked to linger, but she sat resolutely on the chair and smiled at her mother beside her. Face flanked by iron-grey curls, her mother raised her brows and regarded her as if she knew exactly what Hester was about. However, Hester's gambit worked. After a few attempts at conversation, the officer bowed himself off.

"That was almost rude," her mother said, voice hinting of a scold.

"That was as kind as I'm capable of being, at the moment," Hester told her. "The heat is wearing me down. Would you be willing to leave earlier than we had planned?"

Her mother's mouth puckered. "Of course, dear. I'm glad we brought the carriage tonight. Let's collect our wraps and go."

Hester only found a deep breath once they were seated in the coach and heading for Upper Grace, a short distance away.

"That was quite the event," her mother commented, patting down her skirts. "I don't remember the Harvest Ball ever so well attended. Jesslyn must be pleased."

Hester managed a smile at the mention of her brother's wife. "She should indeed. Everyone was there."

Everyone.

She turned her face to the window so her mother couldn't see her smile slipping. Why had he returned? What interest could their little villages possibly hold for him? And who was the pretty blonde at his side in the much-too-fine gown? Sweetheart? Wife?

Why did she care?

"Feeling any better?" her mother asked solicitously.

"I'm sure being home will help," Hester told her.

But it didn't. She couldn't even lose herself in her daughter's warm embrace. Rebecca was sound asleep, golden curls piled up around her face as she lay on her back in her bed, pink lips pursed open.

"Do you think you will be well enough for the fair tomorrow?" her mother asked from where they stood in the doorway of the little room next to Hester's.

The Harvest Fair. She'd forgotten her promise to take her daughter to see the booths and animals. The busy event would be just what Rob preferred.

"I fear not," Hester said. "Perhaps you and Rebecca could go together."

Her mother's lips tightened, but she nodded. "I suppose we must, under the circumstances."

For a moment, Hester's stomach fell as surely as a flock of plovers diving over the Downs. Had her mother guessed? Did she know? But no, the dear lady kissed her cheek as she always did and bade her goodnight before retiring to her own rooms at the end of the corridor.

Odd to feel so guilty after all this time. She'd thought she'd put that summer behind her. She shoved any lingering thoughts firmly away now and made her way to bed.

Somehow, she slept. She was up early enough to dress Rebecca, then stood in the doorway to wave her daughter and mother away from the house as the carriage set out for Grace-by-the-Sea, where the fair was being held. Relief flooded her as she went back inside and shut the door, locking away the world just as she'd once locked away her hopes.

The thought made her stiffen in the entry hall. Rob's defection had sent her to her room for days. Her mother had even called the physician, thinking Hester was sickening. And she couldn't tell either of them that what hurt the most was her heart.

She would not allow him to ruin her life again.

It was too late to call back the coach, and she hadn't ridden in years. They had only coach horses now. She was stuck at home and alone, for even their cook, nursery maid, and upstairs maid had been given the morning off to attend the last day of the fair.

Yet, like a shadow, Rob followed her from room to room. When she glanced out the window at the sunshine, she remembered how the rays had streaked his tawny hair with gold. When she finished sewing a lavender sachet, she remembered the spicy scent of his cologne when he'd bent closer for a kiss.

She set down her sewing work with a sigh and gave in to the memories. What a pair they'd been that summer. She understood now that he'd been looking for fun, attempting to escape his family and the rules of Society. She'd been as willful. Seven years ago, she had just been considered out, and her uncle had been very strict about who she might see, which gentleman might claim her hand in a dance.

"You're a lady, Hester," he'd say. "I'll not have these fellows thinking otherwise."

She hadn't understood the dangers he had feared. Ladies must be treated a certain way—with respect, deference. Other girls seemed to have more fun.

Rosemary certainly did. Their uncle made no pretense

of thinking her someone set on a shelf, too precious for conversation. He'd commissioned a special gown and boots for her so she could follow him all over the area in his search for ancient plants and animals. Rosemary might hike up her skirts and clamber down cliffs. She could spend hours in the sun without being scolded for forgetting her bonnet. Why must Hester only escape the house in the carriage for church?

So, one day, she'd slipped out on her own. She'd told Rob she had climbed out her bedroom window, but that had been as much a fabrication as the name she'd given him. The truth was, her mother had been out shopping, her uncle and Rosemary at their studies. Hester had waited until the cook was busy in the pantry, then edged out the kitchen door and circled the block for the main street of the village.

But of course, nearly everyone along that street knew her family. Even if she avoided her mother, the shopkeepers might remark on seeing her alone, with not even a maid in attendance. Head high, she'd strolled out along the Downs instead, relishing the sun and the breeze that hinted of the seashore only a mile away. She could walk to the shore. She could walk to the spa. She could go anywhere she wanted. The idea was heady.

Voices behind her warned her she had company. Turning, she'd spotted a group of young men not far behind her. Like a pack of puppies, they seemed to be tumbling over each other, laughing, joking, teasing. Her mouth turned up just watching them.

Until they all stopped and stared.

Right. Ladies weren't found alone on the road. What must they think of her?

Her cheeks were heating, but she turned her back on them and continued walking as if they meant nothing. The voices grew closer, until they were on her heels. She refused to speed her steps, though everything in her cried out to run, to escape.

The first fellow passed her on the right with a respect-ful nod. "Ma'am."

Hester nodded in return.

The second edged around her on the left. "Nice day for a walk."

Again she nodded, afraid her voice would come out in a squeak if she opened her mouth.

Three more followed behind him, avoiding her gaze.

The last walked up boldly beside her. "Care for some company?"

Hester caught her breath, taking in the saucy grin, warm gaze, and lean physique. Why, he wasn't even wearing a cravat! She could see the column of his throat between the wilting points of his shirt. She couldn't seem to find her voice.

The first fellow circled back and grabbed his arm. "Sorry, ma'am. He's new to the area, but he meant no disrespect." He tried to tug his friend away.

Rob, being Rob, resisted. "Of course I meant no dis-respect. What's wrong with you, Hugh? The loveliest lass in all the land, and you won't even allow me to say good day?"

The loveliest lass in all the land. She wasn't. But she would have liked to be.

"Don't make a fool of yourself, Charles," his friend countered. "The lady's far above our shoulders."

"Speak for yourself," Rob said. He swept her a bow, arm held wide. "Rob Charles, at your service, my lady. And you would be?"

Introducing himself was so impolite. Her mother would not approve. Her uncle would thunder. The other young men were glancing from him to her to see who would protest first.

Hester held out her hand. "Miss Ascot, of the Wey-mouth Ascots, also recently arrived in the area."

His friend frowned. Like the other lads with him, he hadn't met her, but perhaps he knew her uncle or had seen her in passing. She did her best to ignore him.

Rob took her hand and pressed a kiss to the back. "Miss Ascot. You hold my heart in your palm."

My word.

Her knees had wobbled, and her breath had caught anew, but she'd done her best to keep the haughty smile on her lips as she retrieved her trembling fingers.

"You go on, fellows," he'd said. "I'll just accompany Miss Ascot on her stroll. I wouldn't want her to come upon low company."

That set them all to laughing. With a wave, they'd bounded off for better game.

And Rob had stayed at her side, that day and throughout most of the summer.

Thinking back, she couldn't believe she'd been so brazen. She'd found excuse after excuse to leave the house alone, usually after her uncle and Rosemary had gone collecting. She'd lied to her mother, bribed the maid at the time with pin money, made up stories of friends she must visit, urgent messages she must take to the vicar, anything that might give her a few moments with no chaperone.

Even then, she'd felt a twinge of guilt for hiding her adventures from her family, but that's what time with Rob had been. An adventure, stolen from the rest of her life. Something all her own, something she didn't have to share with anyone.

Only clever Rosemary had suspected. Hester could see it in her sister's eyes when she had come home later than she'd planned and discovered Rosemary already in the bedchamber they had shared. But her sister hadn't questioned her until the day Rob had left, and Hester had come home unable to stem her tears.

Rosemary would understand now. All Hester had to

do was make it to Sunday dinner, when she would have an opportunity to talk to her sister. Sunday morning was challenging enough. Her insides were quaking at church services, but neither Rob nor the lady who had been at his side at the ball showed up at St. Mary's.

Then she had to sit through Sunday dinner with her brother, Larkin, and Jesslyn without blurting out her concerns. But Rosemary, dear Rosemary, again divined something was wrong no matter how hard Hester tried to hide it. She drew Hester aside as they were preparing to return home.

"Has something happened?" her sister asked, clear blue eyes searching Hester's face. "Please tell me you are not worried about me."

"Of course I worry about you," Hester said. "You are my sister. But you are right that something terrible has happened." She glanced to where their mother was hugging Jesslyn goodbye, Rebecca at her side, then lowered her voice. "He's back."

Rosemary's brows went up until they nearly met the line of her warm brown hair. "Rob Peverell has returned? Are you certain?"

Hester nodded. "I quite literally bumped into him at the ball on Friday. Oh, Rosemary! He attempted conversation, and I was horrid to him."

"As well you should be," Rosemary encouraged. "He pretended to be something he was not, raised your expectations, then disappeared without a word. The fellow is a scoundrel."

Hester dropped her gaze, fingers tugging at her glove. "I am not without blame. I pretended to be someone else too, thinking it so romantic. What a fool."

Rosemary took both her hands. "You are no longer that fool. He cannot weasel his way back into your good graces."

Hester managed a feeble smile. "No, of course not."

Rosemary gave her hands a squeeze before releasing them. "The Peverells rarely leave their monstrosity of a house on the few occasions when they are in residence. You probably won't have to face him again."

Now, why did some part of her find that thought disappointing?

He must be mad that he kept thinking of ways to see Hester Todd again. The Harvest Fair was the logical choice. Saturday was the last half day. It was just the sort of place he enjoyed. But Elizabeth was bluedevilled, so Rob remained at the Lodge.

Not that he found the Lodge particularly welcoming. An ancestor had originally built the house of brick imported to the area. Successive generations had added here, expanded there, until it was a sprawling complex with far too many wings and corners. Most rooms and corridors were paneled in dark wood, making the house seem even more like a labyrinth. And now Napoleon's troops were massing just across the Channel, howling for a way across. Not the most congenial of places. Just the one with the fewest memories of his family.

The paperwork his steward brought him that afternoon held memories enough. His father's will left Rob every property—the house in London, the country house in Wiltshire, a hunting box in Scotland, and the Lodge between Grace-by-the-Sea and Upper Grace. All had staff. Some had tenant farmers working the land.

Then there were the investments. He hadn't realized his father had been such a visionary, or perhaps that had been the contribution of his older brother, Thomas, but Rob held stocks in companies that imported tea and silk, built bridges and roads, and constructed machines like a steam engine for transportation. Keeping everything on stable footing depended upon sound judgement.

Something no one had ever praised in him.

"Just one more signature today," his steward, Percival Mercer, said, slipping a sheet of parchment in front of him as Rob sat at his father's desk in the study. "This is the agreement to buy the land that runs from the Lodge down to Grace Cove. Your father would be very pleased you managed to wrest it from Howland after all these years."

Rob glanced up at him. Mercer was a dark-haired, sharp-nosed fellow with a manner far larger than his short stature and slender physique might attest. "And is Lord Howland pleased to have the land *wrested* away from him?" Rob asked.

"Very," Mercer assured him with a smug smile. "The Howland estate is in dire financial circumstances. The Peverell estate, I am pleased to say, is not."

Because of Mercer's recommendations and his father's wisdom. He was his father's son. Surely some of the man's abilities had passed down to him along with the responsibilities.

He signed the deed, and Mercer snatched it off the desk as if concerned Rob would sully the page.

"Are we finished?" Rob couldn't help asking, gaze wandering to the window. The sun was beckoning.

"Nearly," Mercer said, tucking the paper into his black leather portfolio. "I have always looked on it as my duty to keep the viscount apprised of any information that might be of use."

For one ridiculous moment, he thought the man would tell him where to find Hester. He shook the thought away. Mercer had been his father's steward seven years ago, but he and Rob had never spent any time together before his change in circumstance three months ago. He made himself lean back in the stiff leather desk chair.

"And what information have you discovered now?" he asked as if the matter held no concern whatsoever.

Mercer drew himself up. "I have been informed that someone has been docking at the Peverell pier below the Lodge. The ship arrives in the dark of the night and disappears by morning."

Rob raised a brow. "Dark of the moon? Smugglers then."

Mercer eyed him, then licked his flabby lips. "Then my lord has an aversion to smugglers."

Every syllable shouted his doubt. The fellow was right to question him. Once, Rob would have thought it great fun to encourage smugglers, perhaps even to travel with them on one of their illicit runs.

"My lord has no interest in smugglers," Rob agreed as firmly as possible. "James Howland is magistrate now. If we discover anything of use, we'll inform him immediately."

Mercer nodded, though he did not look relieved. "A wise course, my lord. I'll do my best not to trouble you further until next week."

He almost asked why, then remembered. Tomorrow was Sunday, a day he generally spent sleeping late after a night of frivolity. Now he must accompany Elizabeth to services.

They had never attended St. Andrew's in Grace-by-the-Sea with any regularity, so none of the dark box pews bore a brass plaque with the name of Peverell on it. Some part of him whispered he had no business in the little chapel. The Howlands had donated the silver cross on the steeple and the stained-glass windows on one side. They had their own pew near the front. Dressed in their Sunday best, the villagers filled the other pews, exchanging smiles with friends, family, and neighbors. The spa visitors also gathered near the front, gentlemen in fine wool, ladies in silk. Perfume wound through the air like incense.

He ushered Elizabeth into an empty pew near the back. She cast him a glance as if wondering why he didn't claim a spot closer to the altar, with the rest of the wealthier attendees. He could not tell her that he was simply grateful to be here.

And he could seek guidance from the back of the church just as well as the front.

Indeed, he heard little of the service. His thoughts carried heavenward, searching for insights. Thomas had been the oldest, the heir. He'd received all the tutoring in what it meant to be the viscount. On occasion, his father would attempt to interest Rob in family matters. His mother would always wave a hand.

"Stop pestering the boy, Peverell! Our Rob was meant for finer things."

She'd hoped he might join the church. When it was obvious he was unsuited, she'd encouraged a commission in the army. Neither had appealed to Rob. The truth was, little had appealed to him. It was as if he had no purpose, no real place in the world.

You made me for something, Lord. It might not have been this, but this is what I must do now. I could use Your guidance.

The Lord didn't see fit to speak to him. Neither did Elizabeth, until he helped her up into their carriage afterward.

"In such a hurry to leave?" she asked.

He took his seat across from her. "Do I appear to be running away? Dear me. I'll have to try harder."

She shook her head. "You needn't have pelted. Mrs. Todd wasn't there. I looked."

He started. "Mrs. Todd likely attends St. Mary's in Upper Grace."

"Ah." She settled into the seat. "Perhaps we can go there next week. It's just as close to the Lodge by road."

Worship would be even more challenging if Hester

was nearby. "St. Andrew's is visible from the Lodge. It makes more sense to go here."

"As you wish." She tugged down on the cuffs of her grey redingote. "We should make our presence known. We could visit the vicar, tour the spa."

He nodded. "Whatever amuses you."

Her mouth quirked. "Then let's start by seeing the dame school in Upper Grace tomorrow."

"What are you up to, Elizabeth?" he challenged.

Her eyes widened in the look their mother had always called too innocent by half. "Nothing! But if you can enliven a boring summer, I can enliven a boring winter. I'd like to see more of this Mrs. Todd."

He should protest. Nothing good could come of it. Yet, he also wanted to see Hester again, if only to assure himself she fared well.

"As you wish," he repeated and hoped he didn't sound as eager as he felt.

CHAPTER THREE

HESTER WAS GLAD WHEN MONDAY came around, in part because it was easy to slip into her routine and in part because she always felt a tingle of pride when she walked into the school.

Rosemary had envisioned the dame school and developed its curriculum to be the finest in Dorset. Mr. Jenkins, the rector at St. Mary's, had been so impressed with Rosemary's plan that he'd offered her the use of the old coach house behind the church. The church leaders approved the annual budget, which came largely through donations.

So many families had pitched in to clean and refurbish the space. Two of the fathers had built the wood floor, and several of the mothers now took turns seeing to its cleaning and polishing. Other parents had constructed benches, painted the walls a friendly blue, and mounted a chalkboard at one end. Mr. Howland, the magistrate in the area, had purchased primers for reading, and Hester had convinced the local merchants to provide slate boards and chalk for the children to use in copying out their letters and doing their sums.

Rosemary had started as teacher, with Hester assisting her, but some of the fathers had complained to the rector that a young, unmarried woman shouldn't be teaching their sons. So, Hester had been promoted to teacher, and

Mrs. Mance, who kept the rectory here as well as the vic-
arage in Grace-by-the-Sea, came up for part of the three
days the school was in session to assist Hester.

They had fourteen students, counting Rebecca, rang-
ing in age from six to twelve. The school ran all year, but,
from spring to fall, Hester was never sure who would
show up, as many of the children were needed by their
families. Businesses in town must cater to spa visitors or
those coming in for one of its events. Families farther out
from Upper Grace tended crops or animals.

But now, with harvest over and the fair done, all her
pupils crowded into the room to take their places on
the benches. Sunlight coming through the only window
along one wall anointed heads with hair slicked down
and shoulders tight in worn cotton or rough-spun wool.

"Time to begin," Hester announced from the top of
the room.

Fourteen bodies wiggled into position, gazes bright.
Hester clasped her hands in front of her, and they all
mimicked her.

"Dear Lord," she prayed, "bless us and our families
today. Give us ears to hear and eyes to see the goodness
of your world. May we be respectful and diligent in our
work so that we may in turn be a blessing to others.
Amen."

"Amen."

Heads popped up, hands fell. All but one.

Rebecca waved her little fingers over her head.

"Yes, Rebecca," Hester said, trying not to smile.

"May we please read more about *The History of Little
Goody Two-Shoes*?"

Hester had taken to reading to the children every day
around the noon hour. They were very engaged at the
moment in learning what would befall Miss Margery
Meanwell and her brother Tommy as they sought to rise
from being orphaned.

"Later," Hester promised, "if everyone works very hard and finishes their work this morning."

Rebecca dropped her hand and sighed, gaze darting to Jimmy Welton, who cringed even though he was three years older. Jimmy had a problem with paying sufficient attention. If anyone would be late in finishing, it would be him.

Hester started them on spelling, choosing simpler words for the less experienced students and challenging words for the more experienced. While Mrs. Mance listened to their spelling, white hair like the crown of a dandelion around her face, Hester set up a series of arithmetic problems on the board, again segregated by ability. The light darkened a moment, and she glanced up to see a carriage passing close to the building.

Jimmy must have seen it too, for he jumped from his bench and rushed to the window. "Who's that?"

Two more of the older boys followed him to press their noses against the glass.

"Nobody from around here," one of them claimed.

"Look at those horses," the other marveled. "My brother would call them goers."

Their exclamations had an effect on the girls as well. Hester turned as half the class strained to see out. Mrs. Mance even joined them, hands clutching her black skirts.

"That's enough, students," Hester said. "Whoever it is will most certainly not be coming to see us. Return to your benches."

Slumping, with many backward glances, they did as she ordered. Mrs. Mance, however, clung to the window. Before Hester could get everyone focused again, the round little housekeeper hurried to her side.

"It's Viscount Peverell," she hissed.

Rob's father, here?

She must have paled, for Mrs. Mance clutched her arm.

"There, now, he's not nearly as fearsome as his father, God rest his soul. And he could certainly use some kindness, after losing father, brother, and mother in that awful accident."

She felt as if the schoolroom was spinning around her. "Are you saying Robert Peverell now has the title?"

Mrs. Mance nodded. "He and his sister were in church this Sunday. It was the saddest thing you ever saw, the way they sat at the rear as if they were penitents. The vicar has been trying to determine when it might be suitable to go up and comfort them, poor dears."

So, that had been his sister at the ball. Pleasure she did not understand was quickly snuffed by sorrow. He'd lost nearly everyone in his family. As much as Rob had hurt her, she could not wish such a tragedy on him.

"Perhaps he's come to see the rector," she ventured.

"Quite possibly," Mrs. Mance agreed before aiming a frown into the schoolroom. "Ho, Jimmy. Back to your seat now."

Jimmy skulked to the bench even as a knock sounded on the door.

Everyone froze. Hester could hear the tick of a beetle in the wall.

Mrs. Mance licked her lips. "Will you get that, or shall I?"

"Please," Hester managed.

The housekeeper bustled forward, black skirts sweeping the floor. Hester hadn't realized she was holding her breath until her chest began to ache.

"Good morning, my lord," Mrs. Mance warbled. "Miss Peverell. How might we be of service?"

"We heard you'd opened a dame school since last we visited the area."

That must be his sister. She had a clear, sweet voice that rang with conviction.

"We have indeed," Mrs. Mance said, considerable chest

swelling in pride. "Won't you come in and view it?"

Hester took a step forward, as if she could will them out of her space. But of course, that would never work. Rob had ever done whatever pleased him most. Now he and his sister came into her school and made everything seem small.

At least he looked the gentleman today. Tall brown-leather boots and chamois breeches covered his long legs. A bottle-green coat covered his broad shoulders. Why, that top hat wasn't even cocked at a rakish angle, as if he were a proper fellow with a serious nature.

He didn't fool her for a moment.

This time, though, she noticed the touches of mourning. He wore a black armband on the left, and his sister's redingote was a steely grey, as were the skirts peeking out below. Half-mourning, then. Their parents must have been gone three months or more.

Mrs. Mance hurried to join Hester at the front of the room. "This is Mrs. Todd, our teacher," she told their guests. "Hester, dear, allow me to introduce Lord Peverell and his sister."

Hester dropped a curtsey, as propriety demanded, her navy skirts pooling. "My lord, Miss Peverell."

"Mrs. Todd." He held himself back, as if he thought she might break if he approached her.

She might at that.

She turned to her class, all of whom were staring at the pair. "Children, how do we welcome visitors?"

"Good day, Lord Peverell, Miss Peverell," they recited in unison.

She drew in a breath. She could do this.

"Have you come to be our father?" a little voice piped up, brimming with hope.

Hester stared at her darling daughter, looking so yearningly at Rob, and all breath fled.

Rob found it difficult to focus on the angelic looking little girl dressed in soft blue when Hester stood close enough to touch. The severe lines of the navy wool gown did nothing to hide her curves or the pulse beating at the curve of her neck. He kept his hands at his sides and a smile on his face.

"I fear I don't have that honor, young lady," he said. "But perhaps you could help me understand more about your school."

"She has all the luck," someone muttered, but the little one wove her way to his side and stood looking up at him, eyes huge in her creamy face. In fact, she reminded him a bit of Elizabeth when she'd been that age—five, six?

"May I help him, Mama?" she asked, gaze going to Hester.

Mama?

His Gwen had a child.

He felt as if the floor had tilted, pushing him toward the door as if to evict him from her presence. He wasn't aware he'd stepped back until Elizabeth clutched his arm and frowned at him.

"We should all help him, Rebecca," Hester said with a smile to her daughter that set his breath to hitching. "We'll take turns showing Miss Peverell and her brother what we learn here at the Upper Grace Dame School."

Dame school. Never had the appellation been less fitting. Most dames were aged ladies who taught rudimentary skills from their drawing rooms. As the children lined up in front of him and Elizabeth, it quickly became clear that they had learned far more.

And Hester was hardly a dame.

The care she took of her charges was evident by the way

she put a hand on a shoulder to protect, nodded with a smile to encourage. The other lady, who he remembered as Mrs. Mance, the vicar's housekeeper, brought chairs for him and Elizabeth to sit, like the honored guests they were, and then she and Hester took turns ushering groups of children to face them.

One set of two older girls and a lad showed how well they spelled.

"Perspicacious," the blonde said, shifting back and forth in her worn smock. "P-e-r-s-p-i-c-a-c-i-o-u-s."

Elizabeth applauded her, which set her to beaming.

Rob was more pleased with the warm smile that curved Hester's pretty lips. It took little to remember the sweet pressure of those lips against his. He kept his face neutral as another group of three girls began reciting Wordsworth in unison.

"In thoughtless gaiety I coursed the plain,
And hope itself was all I knew of pain.
For then, the inexperienced heart would beat
At times, while young Content forsook her seat,
And wild Impatience, pointing upward, showed
Through passes yet unreached, a brighter road."

He could not stop himself from glancing at Hester, who avoided his gaze. Thoughtless gaiety? Impatience leading the way? Had she been thinking of him when she'd taught them this?

And wasn't that his usual arrogant thinking?

He made himself smile and nod as they finished the portion of the long poem, then curtsied to him.

The three boys in the third group took turns reading from a primer. All too easy for his gaze to wander back to Hester again. Her eyes were on her students, her mouth silently forming the words as if she could will the boys to sound them out. Her students must dote on her.

He found it difficult not to dote on her.

Finally her daughter, Rebecca, and two of the littlest

girls stepped forward to count.

"I can count to twenty," Rebecca announced, twisting from side to side in her pretty blue frock. "One, two, three, four, five, six, seven, eight, nine, ten, eleven, twelve, fourteen…"

"You forgot thirteen," one of the others whispered, giving her a nudge with her elbow.

Rebecca scowled at her. "No, I didn't. I don't like thirteen."

"I'm not overly fond of it myself," Rob told her, while Elizabeth hid a smile.

"Numbers," Hester put in, "are not for us to like or dislike. There is an order to them, and thirteen has a place. Start at thirteen, Rebecca."

Her daughter heaved a mighty sigh. "Thirteen, fourteen, fifteen, sixteen, seventeen, eighteen, nineteen, twenty."

"Excellent work," Rob assured her.

He was so captivated by the way Hester glowed at her daughter's accomplishment that he wasn't certain what the last group demonstrated. He made sure to smile and thank them for their efforts, nonetheless.

"You have all worked hard on your lessons, I see," Elizabeth told them. "Such diligence deserves reward. What would you suggest, Mrs. Todd?"

Hester dropped her gaze. "I'm sure I couldn't say, Miss Peverell."

"I could," Mrs. Mance declared. "Winter's coming on. We've never had a proper hearth. Sometimes we have to cancel classes for weeks because of the chill."

"Well, that's terrible," Elizabeth commiserated. "Don't you think that's terrible, Brother?"

About as terrible as Hester having to raise a child alone. His parents had had nurserymaids, nannies, and tutors for him and Thomas, and a governess for Elizabeth.

"An utter shame," he said. "Would a thousand pounds

resolve the matter, Mrs. Todd?"

Her head snapped up, and her gasp was audible. Her gaze met his, incredulous, grateful.

Wary.

"That is too kind, my lord," she said. "I'm sure it could be accomplished in less than half that."

"But we can use the money for other things," Mrs. Mance hurried to put in. "And thank you so much for your generous donation, my lord."

He inclined his head, but his gaze remained on Hester. Her look challenged him, as if she could see the true motivation behind his gift.

Which was ridiculous. *He* wasn't even sure why he'd offered such a sum.

Elizabeth rose and shook out her skirts. "Thank you all for your warm welcome. I'm sure we'll visit again sometime before we return to London."

Hester directed her gaze at his sister now, and the look was far softer, kinder. For some reason, his chest felt tight.

"Then you don't intend to make the Lodge your home, Miss Peverell?" she asked politely.

"Only through the winter," his sister explained. "But until then, we will have many opportunities to meet. At services, at the assembly, at the spa." She smiled charmingly.

"I regret I'll likely be teaching, but I wish you well," Hester said, smile equally charming but with an edge of determination he could only applaud.

The children stood at attention while Mrs. Mance closed the door behind him and his sister. His last glance of Hester was of her gazing after him, brow puckered as if she simply couldn't understand him.

He knew the feeling.

"A thousand pounds?" Elizabeth asked, picking up her skirts to head for the waiting coach.

"What did you expect?" Rob returned, going to open

the door for her. "You asked to tour the school. Some token of appreciation would generally be expected."

"A token," she said as he handed her into the coach. "Not my quarterly allowance."

"I will not pick your pocket," he promised as he followed her in. "We have plenty for such things."

"I suppose we do." She settled herself and waited until he had done the same and the coach had set out before leaning forward. "Is she yours?"

Hester? Most certainly not. Regrettably. Then he realized his sister was thinking of another pretty lady.

"Rebecca?" he asked, hands braced on the bench. "No. I told you, Hester and I engaged in nothing more than kisses. But if I had had the courage to stay then, she might have been."

Some of what he was feeling must have shown on his face, for his sister reached across the coach to touch his hand. "Was it truly a lack of courage that drove you away from her?"

He sighed. "I have asked myself that question a dozen times over the years. I was young and foolish. I didn't understand the importance of commitment or dedication."

She looked at him askance. "Commitment. Dedication. Such big words, Brother."

"I can spell them too," Rob teased her.

"You should pursue her."

The statement rocked him back in his seat. "Don't be ridiculous. We're still in mourning. I have much to learn about being a viscount let alone becoming a husband and father. And I'm not sure she'd want me."

"She wants you," Elizabeth said.

He shook his head, as if that would clear the thoughts swirling through it. "How can you possibly know? You've met her all of twice."

"And observed her both times," Elizabeth told him.

"At the assembly, you terrified her."

Rob snorted. "Well, that bodes nicely for a courtship."

"Of course it wouldn't," Elizabeth scolded. "But she rallied then, and she rallied today. And, when she thought no one noticed, she looked at you as if you were a lovely bit of buttered toast with jam and she hadn't eaten in days."

"You must stop this conjecture," Rob warned, heart thumping painfully in his chest at the thought of Hester looking at him with such longing. "You know nothing of what she feels."

Elizabeth shrugged. "If she is reticent, which would be perfectly understandable given the circumstances of your parting, you still have your charm. I've never known it to fail you yet."

It had rarely failed, but then it had never encountered a situation as important as this.

"I don't want to cause her any more pain," he murmured. "She's been through entirely enough."

"Oh, Rob."

The admiration in his sister's voice made him raise his head. She was regarding him with a soft, commiserating smile.

"This is the most interest I've seen you show in anything since the accident," she said. "We both could use a diversion, and I think Mrs. Todd could use a friend. Think of this as your second chance to court her."

"And that went so well the first time," Rob reminded her.

She wrinkled her nose at his sarcasm. "This time will be different. This time you have me."

He wasn't sure whether to laugh or leap out of the coach and run as fast as his legs could carry him.

CHAPTER FOUR

A THOUSAND POUNDS! HESTER KNEW many families who would not earn as much in five years' time. As soon as Rob and his sister left, Mrs. Mance grabbed her hands and danced her around the room while the children laughed. Hester's head was still spinning as she walked Rebecca home mid-afternoon at the end of the school day.

Oh, what they might achieve with such funds. Heat for the winter. Supplies to teach the children sewing and elementary woodworking. Perhaps a school garden to tend. Rosemary and their uncle had seen them well-supplied in tomes on botany and animal husbandry, but new books on history and art would really round out the curriculum.

She ought to accept such a gift with grace, but she couldn't help wondering why he would make such an impressive donation. His family hadn't shown any interest in civic concerns in either village before, even though they owned half the land in Grace-by-the-Sea and nearly all of Upper Grace. She could not convince herself this generosity stemmed from some guilt over the way she and Rob had parted.

And if he thought he could buy her good will for a thousand pounds, he was very much mistaken.

She glanced down at her daughter as they walked past

the shops on the main street. Rebecca's hand was firmly in hers, and she swung it as she glanced in the shop windows. Her daughter might only be six, but she'd proven rather observant in the past. Perhaps she'd noticed something that had eluded Hester.

"What did you think of Lord Peverell and his sister, Rebecca?" she asked.

Her daughter screwed up her little face as if thinking took much effort.

"He's tall," she said at last. "And she's pretty. She looks like Esmeralda."

Esmeralda was the latest favorite doll, with flaxen curls and wide eyes painted on her wooden head. She did resemble Rob's sister a bit.

"And why did you ask him about being a father?" Hester pressed.

Rebecca hopped over a crack in the pavement. "I want a father. Everyone else has one."

"Not everyone," Hester allowed as they turned onto the side street that led to her mother's home. "Your uncle Lark, aunt Rosemary and I spent most of our growing up years without a father."

"I still want one," Rebecca informed her. "So does Jimmy."

"Jimmy has a father," Hester said. "He had to go to Portsmouth for work. He'll be back before Christmas."

"Well, maybe mine can come back then too," Rebecca said.

Hester's heart twisted in her chest. "Your father won't be coming back. We've talked about this."

Rebecca sighed as if she remembered the conversation and still didn't like it. "Then maybe Lord Peverell could be my father," she said.

Oh, no. Hester girded herself to explain why Rob Peverell could not be her daughter's father, but Rebecca gave an extra tug on her hand. "Look, Mama! That's Lady

Miranda's carriage."

The Earl of Howland's coach was indeed standing in front of her mother's home. Lacquered to a high sheen, with four perfectly conformed horses standing in the traces, the coach almost made the neat stone house look shabby. Hester hurried Rebecca inside, removed their cloaks and bonnets, and left them on the hall table. They found Rosemary, the earl, and his daughter, Lady Miranda, in the sitting room with Hester's mother.

The earl was a tall fellow whose chiseled features and fair coloring made him resemble his cousin, their magistrate. He'd always looked a bit melancholy to Hester, perhaps because of the death of his father earlier in the year. Today it was as if a candle had been lit inside him, glowing and warm.

As Hester greeted him and her sister, Rebecca went straight to the other girl. "How is your crocodile?"

"Very well," Lady Miranda, who was a few years older, told her. "But we have something more important to tell you. Father is going to marry Miss Denby."

Hester stared at her sister. Pink spread over Rosemary's cheeks as she beamed at the earl. He gazed back at her as if she were the sun come out at the end of winter. Hester had seldom seen a man look so besotted.

"Oh, my dear, how delightful!" their mother cried, hands clasped before her butter-yellow gown. "I'd almost given up hope." She enfolded Rosemary in a hug. The earl looked as if he were trying hard not to grin.

Hester didn't try to hide it. The news was simply too wonderful. As their mother stepped back, she moved in to hug her sister in turn.

"I couldn't be happier for you both," she murmured against her sister's hair. "This exceeds all my expectations."

"Then, perhaps," Rosemary said as she disengaged, "your expectations are too low."

Hester tipped her head in wry acknowledgement, although her sister might not have made the claim if she'd seen Rob at the school today. Best to leave that discussion for another time.

The next little while was all about the happy couple, and everyone was smiling by the time the trio left to announce their betrothal to the earl's family in Grace-by-the-Sea. Though some might say that five months after his father's death was too soon to marry, it was clear there was no real reason to wait. Hester sent Rebecca up to the nursery, where Nurse Peters was waiting.

"How very satisfying to have *one* of you settled," their mother said, perching on the sofa with a happy sigh as Hester came back into the sitting room.

Hester refused to wince. "I am happily settled as well, Mother. I have Rebecca and the school. My life is full."

Her mother cast her a doubtful look. For years she'd been pushing eligible bachelors at Hester—from squires to those who had risen through trade. The wedding might prove an excuse to double her efforts. And Hester didn't want to think what would happen once her mother heard about Rob's generosity to the school.

Such a gift could not be kept quiet in the little village of Upper Grace. Before the school day ended on Wednesday, the rector, the parents, and even her mother had stopped by to marvel. Hester became accustomed to their wondering why, their suggestions on how to use the funds. She was just thankful the news of Rosemary and the earl's betrothal overshadowed the donation at the assembly Wednesday evening.

Grace-by-the-Sea hosted the weekly event in the rooms up the hill from the spa. Her sister-in-law, Jess-lyn, served as hostess. Hester, Rosemary, and their mother hadn't always attended, particularly when the weather was poor, but since her brother Lark had returned to the area this summer, her mother had insisted on going every week, even when her brother's work as Riding Surveyor took him along the coast.

"She'll make a beautiful bride," their mother commented as she and Hester sat along their usual stretch of wall. "See? Even Lord Peverell looks pleased for her."

Hester smiled in agreement, trying not to glance in Rob's direction. She'd noticed him and his sister, standing with the spa set, as she and her mother had entered. Few looked so well in evening black. If her gaze kept straying in that direction, it was because of an appreciation for beauty. No different than what she felt when she gazed at a rosy sunset or viewed one of her friend Abigail's landscape paintings.

She purposely turned her back on him as the musicians tuned up for the opening dance. And there came her first partner, no doubt. Mr. Donner had arrived at the spa earlier this summer and stayed longer than anyone had expected. Tall, dapper, with brown hair, elegant sideburns, and a solid chin, he had persisted in requesting her hand and Rosemary's at the assemblies.

"Mrs. Todd," he greeted her with a bow now, the silver buttons on his dove grey coat catching the light. "Might I hope to partner you this dance?"

"Delighted, sir," Hester said, taking his arm.

She could feel her mother watching and willed her not to comment. Mr. Donner was not an eligible bachelor, to Hester's mind. He had come from London, and he would return one day. She had no wish to be anywhere but here.

He was, however, a reliable partner—always remembering the steps, always there to take her hand and lead her when the dance required. They finished the set, and he returned her to her seat. Rosemary slipped in behind him as he left, fanning herself with one gloved hand.

"I never thought I'd be a seven day's wonder," she told Hester. "Nor have to plan a wedding so quickly. Drake is riding for a special license. We're to be married on the twelfth."

"That's only nine days away," Hester realized. "Mother will have apoplexy."

"We can manage with Jesslyn's help," Rosemary assured her. She pressed something into Hester's hand. "Here. I have a present for you in the meantime. You need them now more than I do."

Hester frowned down at the little pair of glasses on the black satin ribbon. "Why would I need your lorgnette? My eyes are fine."

"So are mine," Rosemary informed her. "These aren't for improving your vision. They are a highly effective shield to keep others from looking too closely."

Is that why her sister had used them all these years? The lorgnette had appeared in her sister's hand shortly after Rosemary had begun helping catalogue their uncle's collection. Hester had assumed the painstaking work had tired her sister's eyes. Strange to think of her brave and clever sister needing a shield.

As their mother returned to her seat as well with a nod to Rosemary, Hester draped the ribbon about her neck. The lorgnette felt odd hanging between her breasts, like a weight on her heart. It didn't seem like much protection.

"Pardon me, ladies."

That voice. Hester closed her eyes a moment before pasting on a smile and turning.

Rob stood just beyond, polite smile on his own face. "Would you care to dance, Mrs. Todd?"

Before she thought better of it, she grasped the lorgnette, lifted it to her eyes, and pinned him through the glass. He shifted on his feet, as if considering running.

How very marvelous.

"The last dance tired me," she told him. "I had thought to sit this one out."

"But you are welcome to sit with us, my lord," her

mother put in.

Rob promptly plunked himself down next to her mother and looked up at Hester expectantly.

"Keep the lorgnette handy," Rosemary murmured before taking herself off to join the earl.

For a moment, Rob thought Hester would find another excuse to avoid him. Then she sighed and sank onto the chair next to his. He caught a hint of spice, like apple cider on a crisp autumn day, before she folded her hands in the lap of her cinnamon-colored gown and pointed her gaze out into the assembly room.

"There's Jesslyn," her mother announced, rising. "I must speak to her. Will you save my seat, my lord?"

"Assuredly," Rob promised even as Hester stiffened anew. He draped an arm over the back of the chair.

The music started. The couples began hopping about. Elizabeth had accepted the arm of a curly-haired fellow who seemed entirely too enthusiastic. Voices hummed all around him and Hester. Crystal chimed as someone must have touched glass to glass.

"How was school today?" he asked.

"Fine."

"I've asked my steward to put the money on deposit at Hazard's bank in Upper Grace," he explained. "You can draw on it whenever you like."

"Thank you."

Why was it so difficult to talk to her? Rob leaned back as far as the chair would allow. "An economy of words, I see. Impressive. What if I were to ask you about your daughter?"

She eyed him. "She's fine as well."

"Your mother?"

"Fine."

"The tree outside your window?"

She frowned. "What tree?"

"The one I imagined you shinnied down to escape your tyrant of a merchant father."

Color flared in her cheeks. "I must beg your pardon, my lord. There is no tree in front of my bedchamber window. There are no merchants in my family. My father was a Riding Officer for the Excise Office, stationed in Kent. He was killed by smugglers when I was a girl. Rosemary and I found him in a bed of flowers of all things."

He could imagine it, the two girls, their father's unseeing eyes. The shock would have been as great as learning of his family's sudden death. He reached out and touched her hand, finding it stiff. "I'm so sorry. That had to have been terrible. Small wonder you made up a fictitious father."

She raised her chin, but she did not pull away. He tried to take comfort in that.

"We came to live with my uncle, Flavius Montgomery. He had rules as to how a lady should behave, and, at times, I felt them too restrictive. Still, I should not have given you a false name."

"And I should have given you the correct one," he acknowledged. "Like you, however, I discovered a certain liberty in pretending to be someone else. My father also had a set of rules I found hard to obey."

She dropped her gaze to where his hand remained on hers. "I understand your father, mother, and brother are gone, now. I'm very sorry for your loss."

"As am I, more than I can say." His throat tightened. "It was such a stupid accident. My father was christening a new pleasure craft on the Thames. The ship collided with another attempting to shoot the tide. Everyone aboard was lost."

She pulled away as her fingers leaped to her lips. "Oh,

how horrid."

The blackness threatened. "It was. Elizabeth and I never expected to find ourselves in this position. We were the spoiled younger children, you see. We were supposed to be exempt from such things."

Her face was sad. "None of us is really exempt from sorrow, I fear."

How well she must know that. "Allow me to express my own condolences on the loss of your husband. He must have been an impressive fellow to capture your heart. A love match, I take it?"

She lifted the lorgnette, and her gaze speared him through it, the blue-green of her eyes sharpened by the glass. "Why would you assume otherwise?"

A dozen reasons came to mind, but she wouldn't like any of them. "I try not to assume. Perhaps you've noticed the danger?"

Too late he realized he had reminded her of the assumptions she'd made about him. He could almost see ice forming on the lens of the lorgnette.

"Did you sit beside me with the goal of asking impertinent questions?" she challenged.

"No," Rob said. "Though I've always been told I'm rather good at them, so I'll thank you not to impugn one of my few useful skills."

"And I'll thank you not to trouble me again." She stood, forcing him to his feet, then dropped her lorgnette and swept away from him.

Nicely done, Rob. And you're supposed to have a silver tongue.

He rose and strolled in the opposite direction, trying not to look as disappointed as he felt. What had he expected, that a gift to the school and a few kind words would have her falling back into his arms? She had been, and still was, a diamond of the first water. If he wanted to restore himself in her good graces, he'd have to work harder.

The curly-haired fellow deposited his sister back at Rob's side after the dance had ended. She didn't seem the least upset when he took himself off.

"Unimpressive?" Rob asked.

"Tolerable," she pronounced. "And what of you? I saw you sitting with Mrs. Todd. Did I detect a thaw in the air?"

"Perhaps a touch of late fall," he allowed. "But winter soon set in again."

She raised a brow. "Could my charming brother be losing his abilities?"

Rob looked down his nose at her. "I have lost only the skirmish. It is far too soon to be declaring the results of the war."

Another fellow approached just then. He'd been the first to claim Hester's hand for a dance, but Rob hadn't detected any particular warmth between the two.

"My lord," he said with a nod. "Miss Peverell. Mrs. Denby, the spa hostess, introduced us at the Harvest Ball."

"Ah, yes, Mr. Donner," Elizabeth said with a smile. "How are you faring?"

"Well enough," he said, "but I could count my night a success if I had an opportunity to dance with you."

Elizabeth sent Rob a look, as if to say this was how it should be done. Really, the fellow was far too obvious with his fatuous smile and manly chin. Still, he returned to the floor with Elizabeth on his arm.

Should he have protested? He hadn't had to involve himself with these sorts of decisions before. His mother had always chaperoned his sister for the seven years she had been out. During that time, Elizabeth had garnered no less than thirteen offers of marriage. She'd managed to convince Father to refuse all of them. That had made for gossip sufficient enough to eclipse even some of *his* antics.

"What is she waiting for?" Rob had heard their mother

lament one night after Elizabeth had gone to bed. "She's refused titles, wealth, position, and power. And she never gives me a better answer than *I didn't care for him*."

"Elizabeth has exacting standards," their father had said, voice heavy with pride. "And my little girl deserves a fellow who meets every one."

His little girl. That had been Elizabeth's role in the family, no matter her age. She was his father's darling, who could do no wrong. Thomas was the dutiful firstborn, determined to please, to excel no matter how high the standard. Rob was the charming entertainment.

And now he must be so much more.

"Good evening, my lord," Mrs. Greer said. The angular blonde giggled as she ventured closer, as if he'd given her a witty retort instead of silence. "I do hope you are enjoying our little assemblies."

"Immensely," he assured her. "And how is your husband the arborist this evening?"

Her smile stiffened. "He is an apothecary, my lord, though you are so healthy you would not require his services, I'm sure. And he is quite well, thank you for asking. Looking forward to his next term as president of the Spa Corporation Council."

"Lord Howland appointed him, then," Rob mused. "Or is that my role as viscount now?"

She drew herself up. "No, indeed, my lord. Every position on the council is elected annually by the entire village. My husband has been elected president for the last six years running. It is an exacting position, requiring patience, fortitude, and wisdom, all of which my husband possesses in good measure."

"Well, I wish him the best of luck," he told her.

The vicar approached them just then, and Mrs. Greer made way for him.

"Mr. Wingate," she said with an equally ingratiating smile. "How fortunate we are to have you attend tonight."

A slight fellow, the minister tended to bob his head when speaking as if agreeing to his own logic. "I came for the express purpose of thanking Lord Peverell for his generous donation to the dame school in Upper Grace. The rector, Mr. Jenkins, could not stop speaking of it when we met earlier this week."

"It is the talk of the village here too," Mrs. Greer assured him, though he had a feeling the news had not reached Grace-by-the-Sea as yet. "A hundred pounds was it?"

"A thousand," the vicar informed her.

She paled, hand going to her heart. "A thousand!"

"A donation befitting the endeavor," Rob told them both, feeling as if his cravat were tightening around his neck.

Mrs. Greer's exclamation had drawn others closer. Before he knew it, they were singing his praises. He was kind, generous, a visionary. He could have told them that even the cruelest villain could donate to a worthy cause if it benefitted him. Rob had never claimed to be a saint.

Just a sinner trying hard to reform.

CHAPTER FIVE

NO FOOTMAN OPENED THE DOOR for them when Rob and his sister reached the Lodge that evening. They had brought only a few servants with them—Elizabeth's maid, Kinsey, and his valet, Eckman, as well as their chef and his favorite assistant. The rest Elizabeth had arranged to hire temporarily from Mrs. Catchpole at the local employment agency. Rob was only surprised the footman did not appear to know his job.

He helped Elizabeth off with her cloak, then turned for the heavy stairs. She hummed to herself as they climbed. While Rob was delighted to see her happy, he couldn't help wondering whether he should have been more attentive to who had partnered her at the assembly.

What if one was a fortune hunter or had lascivious motives? Would Mother have been able to ferret out the truth? On the other hand, he knew how easy it was to maneuver around some mothers, especially those hoping to advance in social standing, no matter the cost. Should he have hired a stern-faced chaperone to attend his sister instead?

"Thinking of Mr. Donner, perhaps?" he asked as they gained the landing.

She smiled, turning to the left down the corridor that beckoned. "Perhaps. I talked with a number of interesting people tonight—Mr. Donner, Lord Featherstone, Mrs. Denby, Hester's mother."

"Hester's mother?" The question came out far too much like a yelp as she wandered into the withdrawing room on that wing.

"Don't get in a pucker," Elizabeth soothed. "It wasn't as if you were much company. You were positively surrounded at times." She went to sit on one of the chairs near the window that overlooked the Channel. The shutters had yet to be closed, and darkness pressed against the glass.

Rob shook his head as he sat beside her. "Amazing what a thousand-pound donation can do."

"Was that all they wanted?" she asked. "To comment on your generosity to the dame school?"

Once again, his cravat seemed to be tightening. He tugged at it with two fingers. "Perhaps at first. I'm sure it didn't help that I agreed to the vicar's proposal."

Her brows went up. "And what did our fine vicar propose? Seat cushions for some of the pews? A donation to the benevolence fund?"

Rob swallowed. "I may have agreed to allow the use of one of our leased properties as a home for widows."

Her eyes widened, then narrowed. "Widows? What sort of widows, precisely?"

"Real widows," Rob assured her hurriedly. "Proper widows. That is, widows I have never so much as met. Oh, leave it be, Elizabeth."

She trilled a laugh and cuffed him on the shoulder.

Truly, he wasn't sure why he'd agreed to allow the use of the house. How many widows in need of supporting could Grace-by-the-Sea have? And why was he the one to support them? Elizabeth was right to question him. It was ridiculous, him a benevolent patron. *He* was ridiculous.

So, why did some part of him feel smugly pleased to

have been of use?

Their temporary footman came hurrying into the room then, bucket in one grip. So, that was why he hadn't been at the door. He must have been carrying coals for the morning fire; his gloves were already dusted with black. A slender fellow with brown hair, he couldn't be much older than twenty. Now he jerked to a stop at the sight of them and bowed his head, deferential to the point of hesitancy.

"Ah, there you are, Bascom," Elizabeth said. "Remind Monsieur Antoine I am hoping for kippers tomorrow morning. In the breakfast room, if you please. I see no reason to eat in that cavernous dining room on the ground floor."

"Yes, Miss Peverell," Bascom said, but his voice cracked.

That might not be because of his youth. Monsieur Antoine ruled his kingdom with raised voice and hurled crockery. Woe betide anyone who failed to bow. His father had praised the man's cooking but left his management entirely to their housekeeper in London. But Mrs. Hurley had stayed to take care of the house there in their absence. Elizabeth was directing the staff while they were in Grace-by-the-Sea.

Still, the footman hesitated, glancing from Rob to his sister as if wondering what he was supposed to do now.

"Don't let us disturb you further, Bascom," Rob told him. "See to your duties."

"Yes, my lord. Thank you, my lord." The young footman edged from the room as if he thought they might take a bite of his grey livery.

"Be patient with him," Elizabeth chided. "He's new to the role."

"He isn't the only one," Rob quipped.

Elizabeth smiled at him, and all at once he became aware of the quiet. It was a momentary reprieve. He had never stayed in a place more conducive to noise.

As the day warmed, the Lodge cracked and popped like an elderly gentleman rising from his chair in a stretch. It made similar protests as night came on and the air cooled. Wind whistled down the chimneys, sang through cracks in the window casings. At a particularly high tide, waves beat on the cliff below and set the entire place to reverberating. He had yet to experience it in a storm. It would likely be akin to sitting in front of an orchestra madly tuning up all at once.

"I should like to visit the spa tomorrow," his sister announced, stretching out her legs. "Say eleven?"

He was expecting his steward any day, with more decisions to be made, but someone could always come for him if Mercer arrived.

"Very well," he said.

"See that you wear something appropriate," Elizabeth ordered.

Rob frowned. "Since when do you comment on my wardrobe?"

She reached out and tweaked his lapel, as if it had been out of place. "Since you decided to turn a new leaf. We must present you in the best possible light. Oh, look. What's that?"

He thought she meant to prevent further questions, but he followed her gaze to the window. Something flashed at sea—blue. Like a prick of a pin in the dark of the night.

Smugglers.

Excitement tingled up his back. A shame he must be the viscount now. What he wouldn't give for a little adventure.

Then again, why shouldn't he make sure his home was safe?

"I'm sure it's nothing that need concern you," Rob said, purposely turning from the view. "You must be tired from all that dancing. I won't keep you any longer. Good night, Elizabeth."

She scowled at him. "You know something. I won't be left out, Rob. What was that? What do you intend to do about it?"

If only he had his father's ability to demand obedience. Then again, Elizabeth had never bent, even to their father.

"I understand smugglers may have been using the pier below the Lodge," he explained. "That flash was a beacon asking whether it is clear to come in. Someone may be out on the property now, answering."

"And you intend to face him down," she accused. "I won't let you go alone. Give me a moment, and I'll fetch Thomas's dueling pistols."

He stared at her. "Thomas dueled?"

"Only once," she assured him primly, "and he didn't hit his opponent."

Rob shook his head in disbelief. "And I suppose you know how to load them."

She nodded. "I asked Father to show me."

This night was only getting stranger. "No need to fetch them. Bascom can come with me."

"Bascom would hop up on a chair if a mouse appeared," she informed him. "You have only to look at him to know that."

She might be right. Rob stood. "I'll send him for Fitch and his stable hands, then. That ought to give our smugglers a start."

"I'm coming too," she insisted.

He decided to stop fighting. If his mother and father had been unable to convince her to behave with propriety over the past six and twenty years, why would his feeble arguments bear any weight?

A short time later, Mr. Fitch, two stable hands, and Bascom gathered with Rob and Elizabeth on the small narrow stretch of lawn that ran from the stables and coach house at the east end of the headland to the coal shed and an outbuilding where his father had stored boating gear on the west. Along the edge, the land dropped steeply to the shore. The sea breeze set the trees to swaying in the moonlight, but Rob heard nothing except the faint rustle of the leaves and the shush of the waves.

"Caught no sign of anyone from the stables, my lord," his coachman declared, raising his lantern as he scanned the area. "Or when we crossed the lawn."

"I saw nothing from the house," Bascom put in.

"The flash was there," Elizabeth said. "Rob and I both saw it."

Rob stepped farther onto the grass, senses tuned to any sound, any movement. A bird wheeled across the moon, then dove for the waves. A rabbit bounded for cover among the bushes closer to the house.

With Elizabeth and his staff at his back, he worked his way out to the edge of the cliff, until he could see the pier jutting into the water. Grace Cove around the turn of the headland was sheltered, but not quite deep enough for the heavy-bottomed craft his father had favored. Because the headland sank deep under the water here, theirs was the only pier along the entire stretch of coastland.

But it stood empty.

He straightened. "They must have landed elsewhere."

"Good, then," Elizabeth said.

"Aye, and good riddance," Fitch muttered.

Bascom shivered, but Rob didn't think it had anything to do with the cool night air.

"Keep a lantern burning at the back of the house all night," Rob advised, "so a visitor cannot mistake that someone's in residence. I'll ask our steward to see about hiring a night watchman."

"Very good, my lord," Bascom said, brown hair beginning to stick out from where he must have pomaded it in place around his lean face. "I'm sure Mrs. Catchpole will be happy to help."

Rob inclined his head and turned to follow his sister back to the house, Bascom just behind, while Fitch and his assistants headed for the stables. Rob had never had a run-in with smugglers during his wild summer at Grace-by-the-Sea, but he couldn't afford the association now. It might seem like a jolly adventure, but Hester's story of how her father had been killed only chilled him.

He would have to inform the magistrate about the blue light in the morning.

Hester couldn't help the guilt that tugged as she rode home in the carriage with her mother that night. It should have been easy to treat Rob with disdain after what he'd done. Yet his talk of his family's death and the way he'd listened to the story of her father's murder had set her defenses to crumbling.

And that she could not allow. Losing him once had nearly destroyed her. She was not about to fall under his sway again. This time it wasn't only her emotions at risk. She must think about Rebecca. Her daughter deserved a mother who was attentive and not fretting about what might be.

"Lord Peverell seems to have matured into his title," her mother commented as the coach crossed the Downs for Upper Grace. "I remember the stories told of him when he was younger."

Hester tensed. "Stories?"

Her mother's smile was kind. "A young man with time and money on his hands can find too many ways to get into trouble. Racing horses, gambling. And I daresay a few hearts were broken along the way."

Hers certainly had been. "And you think him changed?" Hester asked.

"He will have to change," her mother said, as if decreeing it would make it so. "He's the viscount now. He must secure the line and protect his sister."

And likely in that order, in her mother's mind. Rob had gone from questionable second son to title holder. All over England, matchmaking mamas must be salivating.

Even hers.

"I doubt Lord Peverell will be here long enough for us to find out," Hester said, turning her gaze out the window. "The Lodge was only a passing fancy for anyone in his family."

She hoped that would be the last of it. Her mother must realize one of the costs of marrying into the Peverell family. She'd never wanted any of her children more than an hour's ride away. How she'd worried when Lark had left home to follow in their father's footsteps and become a Riding Officer in Kent. She'd been over the moon with delight when he'd settled down in Grace-by-the-Sea and married Jess.

If Rob and Hester ever worked through their differences and married, Hester might have to travel to Wiltshire and London. She might not see Grace-by-the-Sea more than once every five years.

But her mother merely clasped her hands in her lap. "I suppose we'll see," she said. "In the meantime, I need your help. Nine days is a terribly short time to plan a wedding, especially one to so important a person as the earl. We must consult Jesslyn."

"With Rosemary staying with her and Lark until the wedding, I'm sure she and Jesslyn will have everything planned by the time we see them for Sunday dinner," Hester told her.

"Sunday is entirely too late," her mother insisted. "We will visit the spa tomorrow, at eleven."

Hester frowned as the coach rumbled into Upper

Grace. "But I planned to spend the day working on a new gown for Rebecca. She outgrows them so quickly."

"Perhaps we might go for no more than an hour or two," her mother allowed. She pressed a hand to her chest. "I was so looking forward to a dose of the healing waters."

Fear poked at her. "Are your chest palpitations returning, Mother?"

"Not like the last time," she assured her, lowering her hand. "But perhaps a flutter now and then. Doctor Chance and the waters were so efficacious eight years ago. I'm sure Doctor Bennett will know what to do now."

Hester nodded. "Then of course I will accompany you."

Even if she had to face down Rob in the process.

Though he probably wouldn't be there, she consoled herself as they set out in the carriage the next morning. He hadn't frequented the spa before. Even if he'd grown wiser with age, why would he show up now?

Lark had been the one to accompany her mother eight years ago, leaving Hester and Rosemary with their uncle. Rosemary had kept busy with her studies, but Hester had worried. A heart was nothing to toy with. That her mother's might be failing had kept her up several nights in a row. But the daily doses of the spa water and the change in diet and exercise Doctor Chance had prescribed had done wonders for her mother then. Surely it would be no different now.

And her mother was right. They had much to discuss with Jesslyn about Rosemary's wedding.

Any concerns she had were hard to maintain as they walked into the spa. It was such a welcoming place, with pale blue walls, an elegant bronze wall clock, and columns interspersed between potted palms. White wicker chairs here and there encouraged attendees to sit and chat or gaze out the windows looking down to the cove.

The tinkle of water in the stone fountain in one corner was offset by the music from the white-lacquered harpsichord in the other. Voices murmured in conversation that was punctuated by laughter.

Jesslyn came to greet them the moment she spotted them. "Mother Denby, Hester, what a lovely surprise. How might I be of assistance?"

"We must talk about Rosemary's wedding, dear," her mother said. "But first, perhaps a glass of your fine water."

"And Mother mentioned seeing Doctor Bennett," Hester added with a glance around the spa, looking for the lanky physician.

"Oh, that won't be necessary," her mother said with maddening calm. "I feel better just being here." She nodded to Lord Featherstone, who was making his way toward them through the other guests.

"Aunt Maudie will finish playing shortly," Jesslyn said even as the music shut off with a crescendo of sound. "I'm sure she would be glad to pour you a glass."

Her mother set off across the room. Jesslyn's aunt, Maudlyn Tully trotted to meet her. Lord Featherstone changed directions to join them as well.

Hester shook her head watching as the two older women and the baron exchanged pleasantries. "I begin to believe I've been duped."

Jesslyn frowned. "Why? What's happened?"

"Mother insisted on coming today. First, she worried about the wedding, then she claimed she wasn't feeling well and needed to see the physician. She implied it was her chest again."

Jesslyn paled. Her late mother had been hostess eight years ago when Hester's mother had first had trouble with palpitations, but Jesslyn would remember that time. That's when she and Lark had first met.

"Doctor Bennett has an opening at half past eleven," she told Hester. "Do you think she would consent to be seen?"

"I would feel better if you could convince her," Hester assured her.

Jess nodded. "Consider it done. I know Lark will worry too if we don't. And Rosemary, of course, even in the midst of the preparations."

Hester smiled. "I knew it. She's already asked for your help, hasn't she."

"Well, she has a short time to prepare," Jess said, sharing her smile. "I understand Lord Howland rode for London this morning. While his staff is at her disposal, the bulk of the planning will fall on Rosemary."

"Mother and I are ready to help as well," Hester said. She glanced across the room to where her mother and Lord Featherstone were drinking the water Jess's aunt had handed them. Aunt Maudie, as she had asked Hester and Rosemary to call her recently, was a small older woman who tended to dress all in black. She had a way of pronouncing doom and gloom as well. She'd lost her sailor husband early in their marriage and retreated into fancy. Hester sometimes envied her that ability.

"I could use your help in the meantime," Jess said, leaning closer. "What do you think of Lord Peverell?"

Her mouth went dry. She slowly moved her gaze to Jess and prayed nothing in it would betray her. "What do you mean?"

"You know I'm a matchmaker at heart," Jess said, blue eyes shining with purpose. "A young, wealthy, handsome, titled gentleman in the area is simply too good to forego. What sort of lady do you think he might prefer?"

She fully intended to protest that she had no idea, but words popped out of her mouth before she thought better of them. "Titian haired, the brighter red the better, even if the color comes from a bottle. Ample curves well displayed. Someone who appreciates the more vivid colors—flame, chartreuse, goldenrod. Who guffaws at even a minimum of wit. And no one terribly intelligent."

Jess's brows went up. "Truly? I don't know whether we've ever had a gentleman who preferred his ladies so… obvious."

"Well, then he shall be your challenge," Hester said, nose coming up.

Jess tapped her chin with one finger as if keeping time with her thoughts. "Strange. He struck me more as a gentleman who would value honesty, character, and kindness."

"No," Hester said. "He didn't strike me that way at all."

Jess dropped her hand. "Well, a challenge, as you say. That's why I could use your help."

"Me?" Hester took a step back. "I'm no matchmaker."

"No," Jess allowed, "but you are a good listener. Rosemary and Lark have always said so. Perhaps you could talk to him, ferret out the true Lord Peverell."

She could not know what she was asking. "I doubt I could determine the true Lord Peverell. Besides, our paths are not likely to cross often enough for any serious conversation."

Jess grinned at her. "You might be surprised. He just walked in."

CHAPTER SIX

ROB WASN'T SURE WHY HIS sister had been so determined to visit the spa that morning, but he couldn't believe his good fortune. Hester stood not far inside the door, dressed in a blue redingote the color of the Channel before a storm, misty green skirts peeping out below. Beside her was a tall table with a massive book open upon it. He seemed to recall his father mentioning a Welcome Book, which listed all who had come to the spa. If only he could count on a welcome from Hester.

The magistrate, James Howland, certainly hadn't been welcoming when Rob had gone to see him that morning. A tall, muscular fellow with short-cropped blond hair and a commanding presence, he'd listened as the two had met in his study in his home near the church, and Rob explained the rumors of smugglers and the blue light at sea.

"We had some trouble with smugglers earlier this summer," Howland admitted, leaning back in his chair behind a desk that was far less cluttered than Rob's. "That gang was routed, and I haven't heard of another moving in. But I'll let Larkin Denby, our Riding Surveyor, know about your concerns. He can post someone to keep an eye on your pier."

"I'll take care of that," Rob told him.

Howland nodded. "Very well. Just see that you report

any further trouble to me."

Rob wasn't used to taking orders any more than Elizabeth was, but he could see the wisdom of it this time. Still, something about the way the magistrate watched him, as if measuring him for a new suit or assessing his character, made him wonder what else the fellow knew about trouble in the area. The mighty Howlands had ever tolerated the Peverells when the two families had happened to be in the area at the same time. Was something more afoot this time?

Now Elizabeth drew in a deep breath beside him, as if finding the Grand Pump Room soothing. "How lovely. And so many people for this time of year. I wonder if we'll find anyone we know."

Rob tore his gaze off Hester. "Looking for Mr. Donner?"

Elizabeth widened her eyes. "Donner? Why, I suppose he might be here. Oh, look. There's Mrs. Todd."

He didn't resist as his sister led him to the desk.

The spa hostess, the younger Mrs. Denby, smiled prettily at them. "Miss Peverell, my lord. Welcome. We were just talking about you."

Hester went rigid, which only raised his curiosity.

"Oh?" Elizabeth asked, glancing between them.

The color was draining from Hester's face. How could he help her? Perhaps by taking the attention off her.

"Wondering how to reach my tailor to copy my stunning coat?" he asked, flipping the dun-colored tails for effect.

Mrs. Denby laughed. "Your coat is quite exceptional, my lord, but no."

"I should leave you to your duty, Jesslyn," Hester put in, only to pick up her skirts and rush across the room as if hounds were nipping at her heels.

"I tend to have that effect on her," Rob told the hostess as Elizabeth frowned after Hester.

Mrs. Denby cocked her head, golden curls catching the light. "And why would that be, sir? You seem to have a ready address and a polished demeanor. And there is the matter of your stunning coat."

Rob chuckled. "Your point, Mrs. Denby. I seem to have put myself on Mrs. Todd's bad side."

She straightened. "I wasn't aware Mrs. Todd had a bad side. Hester is known for her warm heart and sweet character."

"I'll speak to her," Elizabeth offered. Without waiting for Rob's reply, she headed toward the fountain, where Hester had joined her mother and Lord Featherstone. The three smiled and spoke, as if they were old friends come to reacquaint themselves. An older woman, Mrs. Tully, if he remembered correctly, swooped away from them like a raven and swung in his direction.

"And what brings you to my spa today, my lord?" Mrs. Denby asked. "Introductions? Interests?"

The questions were said in a honeyed voice, but he heard the stone beneath them. She expected candid answers. Something inside him was determined to give them to her.

"My sister expressed a desire to join your company," he said. "But I begin to think I had another reason for accompanying her." He leaned closer. "Could you convince Mrs. Todd to go riding with me this afternoon?"

As soon as the words left his mouth, he wanted to call them back. He was the viscount. His thoughts must be lofty, learned. His time should be spent improving his properties, his family, and his nation. So why was his gaze once more drawn to the lady laughing over something his sister had said?

He glanced back at the hostess to find her smiling at him, as if she knew better than he did why he'd made his request.

"I fear it's too late in the day for such plans," she commiserated. "Besides, Mrs. Todd and her mother no longer own riding horses, only a pair to pull their coach. You would have to rent one from the livery stable or bring one of yours to town for her."

Disappointment bit sharply. "Yes, of course. I have heard it said I tend to be too impetuous."

"Impetuosity can be its own reward," Mrs. Tully said, joining them. "So can pixie dust."

Pixie dust? Rob grinned at her. "Right you are. I could use some of that about now. Any idea where it could be found?"

She leaned closer, grey eyes bright. "For the right inducement, I could lead you to it."

"Lord Peverell has no need for pixie dust, Aunt," Mrs. Denby told her, though she was smiling too. "Like Lark, he knows the value of spontaneity. But I'm not sure his oldest sister has learned that lesson yet."

Her aunt nodded, grey curls bouncing. "Far too cautious. But she is a teacher. She values learning."

They were both regarding him now. What exactly were they encouraging him to do? Half the things he used to enjoy and could teach would thoroughly disrupt the peaceful spa, and most would destroy any progress he'd made with Hester.

"Who could possibly teach the teacher?" he countered.

Mrs. Denby fluttered her lashes. "Why, a gentleman who was hoping she might want to learn more about him."

Rob couldn't help his chuckle. "Do you number matchmaking among your skills, Mrs. Denby?"

"The mermaids claim she has some facility," Mrs. Tully acknowledged while her niece blushed.

"And I am very fond of both my sisters-in-law," the spa hostess added. "I'm sure you've heard Rosemary Denby is to marry the Earl of Howland next week, my lord."

"It was the talk of the assembly last night," he agreed.

"Even the mermaids have mentioned it," Mrs. Tully put in.

"The earl plans to marry by special license," Mrs. Denby explained, "so there's no need for the three weeks to call the banns. They will be married here at St. Andrew's, with the wedding breakfast to follow in the assembly hall. I imagine there will be dancing afterward."

She waited, and he realized she had a purpose in telling him all this.

"As the head of the other major house in the area, I suspect I will be obliged to attend," he mused.

"Very likely," she said as Mrs. Tully nodded as if he had been very clever.

But her niece still waited, expecting him to come to some conclusion based on their discussion. She would have made as good a teacher as Hester.

"I should also provide the bride and groom with a gift to acknowledge their union," Rob said.

"There's always that pixie dust," Mrs. Tully reminded him. "I should be able to negotiate a very good rate. Your first-borne son, perhaps?"

"I'm sure a gift would be appreciated," Mrs. Denby said with a look to her aunt. "Hester might have suggestions."

Rob's smile curved up once more. He could only bless the woman's intuition and willingness to interfere. "I'll be sure to ask her."

"Excellent," she said. "And do remind her that she promised to help me with a matter. She can start by taking you and Miss Peverell on a tour of the village, so you can find the perfect gift."

They were colluding against her. Hester could find no other explanation for this sudden interest in her activities. Her mother, Jesslyn, even Rob's sister, Elizabeth, were conspiring to throw her and Rob together. They could not know the damage that might cause.

As Lord Featherstone excused himself from their company, Rob sauntered over to them, a cat prowling his domain. Her mother was quick to greet him.

"Lord Peverell, how nice that you would accompany your sister to the spa. A gentleman who puts the needs of family first is always to be commended. Don't you agree, Hester?"

"Certainly," Hester said, willing to give him that.

"I live to serve," Rob assured her. "And, at the moment, I am hoping to be of service to our lovely hostess, your daughter-in-law, I believe, Mrs. Denby."

"Indeed she is," Hester's mother said with a proud look to where Jesslyn was greeting a gentleman and lady who must be Newcomers. Aunt Maudie had created the taxonomy. New arrivals were Newcomers, longtime patrons Regulars. Hester and her mother fell in the third category—Irregulars, having come often enough to be remembered.

"The other Mrs. Denby," Rob said with a look to Hester, "has requested that you reacquaint my sister and me with this fair village."

Had she indeed. More collusion. Hester clamped her lips shut, but her mother pressed a hand to her chest. "What an honor! A shame I haven't been feeling well. I'm sure Hester can guide you."

Hester might not be as clever as her sister, but she would not be outwitted. She slipped an arm about her mother. "But, Mother, I wouldn't want to leave until I know what Doctor Bennett has to say."

"Is it something serious?" Elizabeth asked with concern.

"No, no," her mother hurried to assure her. "But it's always wise to take precautions."

"Yes, of course," Elizabeth said. "Rob, we should not inconvenience Mrs. Todd today."

He inclined his head, and Hester nearly sagged in relief.

"Saturday, then," he said.

"Saturday?" Hester squeaked.

"I believe you teach on Friday," he explained with all solicitation. "And I would not want to interfere with that."

"Being such a patron of the school," her mother added.

Oh, but they were pouring it on thick!

"And I would not want to interfere with your duties, my lord," Hester said. "As viscount, you must have many important things to do."

"True," he allowed, chin up as if he bore his burdens well. "But none more important than this. Without knowing more about the village, how can I find the perfect wedding gift for your sister and the earl?"

Of course, that made her mother gush about his generosity all over again.

Across the room, Aunt Maudie began playing a Mozart sonata on the harpsichord. The spritely music did nothing to soothe Hester's frustrations. Why would Rob need to give Rosemary and the earl anything? The Howlands and the Peverells were not accorded bosom beaus, and Rosemary certainly didn't consider him a friend.

But perhaps Lord Howland would feel compelled to invite Rob and Elizabeth to the wedding rather than slight the only other landed family in the area. Her sister might not like the idea, but she wouldn't be able to protest aloud without sharing Hester's secret, and that Rosemary would never do.

Just then, Doctor Bennett came out of one of the examining rooms at the back of the spa. A tall, studious fellow with warm brown hair, he had married her friend Abigail last month.

"Oh, there's the physician," her mother caroled. "Excuse

me." She headed for his side.

"And there's Mrs. Greer," Elizabeth said, craning her neck as if to catch the attention of the Spa Corporation Council president's wife. "I must go speak to her. I'll be back shortly."

She hurried off before Hester could protest.

Rob leaned closer, until she caught the scent of the spicy cologne he wore. "I believe they are attempting to play matchmaker," he murmured.

"I believe they are quite mad," Hester countered.

He chuckled as he straightened, gaze going toward the windows as if he were fascinated by the little horse-shoe-shaped cove below the village. "I take it your mother isn't aware of our connection."

"We have no connection now," Hester scolded, careful to keep her voice low. "And no, I didn't tell her about that summer. Only Rosemary knows."

He turned to offer her a smile that would once have set her heart to fluttering. "Then I suspect I will need to purchase a very large gift indeed."

"Do you really require my help?" Hester asked.

He wrinkled his nose, making him look years younger. "Alas, I am woefully unprepared for such a duty. And you will know your sister far better than I do."

There was that. And she knew a little something about the Earl of Howland as well. Few in the area realized that his father had left the family finances in a precarious position. Rob could afford to be generous. Perhaps she should help, for her sister's sake.

"Then I suppose we will have to meet on Saturday," she said. "Would you be willing to come to Upper Grace and fetch me around eleven? That would save my mother having to go out in the carriage."

He glanced toward the row of examining room doors, all closed now. "Then that wasn't a ruse. Is she truly unwell?"

The thought plunged a knife in her heart. Hester managed a shaky breath. "I certainly hope not. She claimed chest palpitations this morning. That's why we came. It's happened before, about eight years ago. But she's been fine since."

His hand touched her arm, a brief caress, but she felt it to her toes. "I'm sure the doctor will know what to do."

"I hope so," Hester murmured. "I don't want to lose her."

"I know. I suppose even as an adult, we often think our parents will be there for us forever."

The pain in his voice wrapped around her, and Hester lay her hand over his. "Until they aren't."

"Exactly." He traced a circle on the back of her hand, sending tingles through her. "My father and I butted heads on occasion, but he always tolerated my foibles. Elizabeth and I could do as we pleased, knowing someone would always be there to clean up any messes. Now, I'm not expected to have any messes to clean up. It's quite a challenge."

A smile tugged at her mouth. "But you have always risen to challenges, my lord."

His gaze lifted to brush hers, as briefly as his caress, but just as potent. "Some challenges are more pleasurable than others."

Oh, but she could lose herself in that smile. "And some make us stronger, better able to meet future challenges."

He chuckled. "So, am I to expect choppier waters ahead?"

"Perhaps not," Hester allowed. "Grace-by-the-Sea is known for its sheltered cove, its warm welcome."

"And will I find a warm welcome here?"

She should not give him hope there could be anything between them. He claimed to be trying to change and become the man his father had been. She had seen little evidence as of yet. Still, some part of her grieved with him, sought to comfort him.

"I'm sure you have already felt a welcome," she told him. "You are the other major landowner in the area, after all. And you have been rather generous."

"Which means they welcome me for fear I might take offense otherwise," he pointed out. "That's not a true welcome. What about friendship, camaraderie?"

"I suspect," Hester said, "you are most likely to find that in the new Lord Howland. The two of you have much in common, being recently elevated to the title. Which brings us back to our goal of selecting the best present."

As if sensing she meant to end their conversation, he dropped his hand and stepped back. "Eleven sounds perfect. I'll come for you then."

Hester gave him directions to the house, but she had a feeling she would be counting the hours until Saturday at eleven.

CHAPTER SEVEN

R OB ADJUSTED HIS CRAVAT AS the coach pulled up in front of a three-story stone house off High Street in Upper Grace. The front yard was edged by shrubs, leaves curling and brown with autumn.

"If you touch that linen again," Elizabeth warned from across the coach, "it will wilt off your neck."

"Be nice," he returned as Bascom jumped down to open the door for him. Rob climbed out and followed the short walk to the door. It opened before he could knock.

Hester, her daughter, and her mother stood in the small entry hall. All were dressed in warm colors—russet and orange and peach. The little girl gazed up at him, mouth curving in a shy smile. Rob wiggled his fingers at her. She blushed and ducked behind her grandmother.

"It was very kind of you and your sister to request Hester's help in finding a present for Rosemary and the earl, my lord," Mrs. Denby said, smiling at the coach as if to include Elizabeth. "Would you be willing to join us for tea after you bring Hester home?"

"We'd be delighted," Rob assured her with a bow.

Hester sent her mother a look, but she accepted his arm to walk out to the coach. Rob helped her in, and Bascom hopped up into his place again. As Rob climbed in after Hester, however, he noticed she'd seated herself facing backward, the position generally reserved for a gentleman or a servant. He should insist she sit beside Elizabeth in the forward-facing seat, but he couldn't quite convince himself to forego the pleasure of having her beside him.

So, he settled himself next to her. She frowned at him, but she didn't protest aloud.

The coach lurched as it started away from the house, and her shoulder brushed his. Definitely the best seat in the coach.

Hester was as composed as always. "Good afternoon, Miss Peverell," she said.

"And to you, Mrs. Todd," Elizabeth said with a nod. "But I am certain we are destined to become great friends. Therefore, you must call me Elizabeth."

She turned right enough that he could see her cheeks turning pink inside her straw bonnet. "Thank you, Elizabeth. Then you must call me Hester."

"Excellent, Hester," Rob said.

She had not given *him* permission, but he saw no reason to stand on ceremony. Still, the look she sent him said she knew what he was about.

Elizabeth's smile was amused. "I'm delighted you could join us today. I've heard so much about the shops at Grace-by-the-Sea, but I haven't visited in years. What are our choices?"

"They are many and varied," Hester told her, shoulders coming down in her russet redingote. "But you'll see for yourself soon enough. Perhaps we should stop near Church Street and walk down toward the cove. That would give you a good tour of the area."

"Have you lived here all your life, then?" Elizabeth asked as the coach left Upper Grace and headed out across the Downs like a ship through the tossing waves of the browning grass.

"Since I was a girl," Hester admitted. "We moved here

after my father died to live with my uncle, Flavius Montgomery."

Elizabeth's brows went up. "The famed naturalist? How marvelous. What he must have taught you."

Jealousy crawled up him. Hester had mentioned her uncle before, but the name had meant nothing to him. Figure on Elizabeth to be the better read and more informed.

"He and my sister Rosemary were closer," Hester said, gloved hands folded primly in her lap. "She loved searching for natural curiosities as much as he did."

"Which is why she discovered this ancient crocodile I've been hearing about," Elizabeth mused.

"Actually, Lady Miranda discovered it," Hester said, "and she is rather proprietary about the skeleton, ugly thing that it is. Rosemary tells me Lord Howland intends to make a museum in the castle to house their treasures."

A museum? Well, at least Rob wasn't the only one who felt the need to donate things. Perhaps it was the lordly thing to do.

"Excellent," Elizabeth declared. "I didn't have an opportunity to see it at the fair. We must go visit his lordship, Brother."

"Certainly," Rob agreed. "After the fellow returns from his honeymoon. I imagine he'll have other things on his mind before then."

They must have been starting down the hill into Grace-by-the-Sea, for the carriage tilted just a bit. Once more, Hester was jostled against him. He could get used to that.

He called up to Mr. Fitch, who stopped the coach near the intersection of High Street and Church Street. Bascom jumped down again, but Rob refused to give up the luxury of holding Hester's hand as she alighted. His new footman wore a slight frown as they set out, as if he wasn't sure what his duties were and whether he was performing them adequately.

Elizabeth certainly saw no need to correct him. Head
high, she set off without a backward look, leaving Rob
to offer his arm to Hester. Hester lay down her hand so
gingerly he might have been one of the aged pensioners
come to take the waters. But at least she was content in
his escort. He should be thankful for small favors.

Yet he couldn't help wondering what else he might
do to thaw this wall of ice between them. He had spent
most of his time in the past in Upper Grace, so the village
before him was a strange land. Then again, he was the
stranger. Newcomers, didn't they call visitors at the spa?

"I think you may like this first shop, Elizabeth," Hester
called.

Rob looked up at the sign over the door. "Mr. Carroll's
Curiosities?"

"A veritable treasure trove," Hester promised.

Bascom darted around them to hold open the door,
and Rob followed Hester and Elizabeth inside.

The place was part bookstore, part bazaar, with brightly
colored cases filled with books for children and adults
alike. Tables positioned here and there carried fascinating inventions like miniature automatons, telescopes,
and a model of the famous pyramids in Egypt. Unless
he missed his guess, the massive stuffed creature in the
corner was supposed to be a hippopotamus.

A slight fellow with silver-rimmed spectacles came forward from the back, balding pate shining as brightly as
his smile. "Mrs. Todd. How nice to see you again. And
you brought friends."

Hester didn't quibble the word. "Lord Peverell and his
sister are visiting us for a time. I thought they would
enjoy seeing your collection."

Like a magician on the stage, he stepped aside and
waved his hand. "It is all at your disposal."

The fellow had no idea what he offered. Rob could
spend considerable time and money here. That brass-

rimmed telescope, perhaps, for peering out at strange lights at sea? Or that set of tiny building blocks, which might be assembled into the shape of the Tower of London? Elizabeth was clearly enthralled with a mechanical parrot that made rough noises and bobbed its head when wound by a key.

A shame Rob hadn't come into Mr. Carroll's Curiosities out of, well, curiosity. He was here as a peer of the realm, seeking to honor the wedding of another peer of the realm. And he couldn't imagine Howland beaming over a set of blocks, worse luck.

The dapper shopkeeper brought Hester a tiny cloth bonnet adorned with silk roses. "For Esmeralda?" he suggested.

"Oh, perfect!" Hester opened her reticule and handed him a coin.

"Esmeralda?" Rob asked, joining her even as Mr. Carroll went to pull down a book for Elizabeth.

"Rebecca's favorite doll," Hester said, smiling at the little bonnet.

For a moment, he remembered a similar fond smile being directed at him. Rob shook himself.

"Do you see anything that might please the earl and your sister?" he whispered.

She lowered the bonnet. "Many things, but nothing useful."

Useful. Was that her criterion? He'd thought wedding gifts to wealthy earls should be about beauty, enjoyment. At least, that's the sort of wedding gift he would have preferred. He could imagine Hester opening the gilt paper, eyes wide as she beheld crystal goblets from Ireland or a fine tooled leather portfolio from Morocco.

And when had he started picturing Hester as his bride?

He focused on their task. He knew little of the earl, but Mercer had mentioned Howland might be in financial trouble. If that were true, what need had the earl for more baubles? Rob must consider something of more substance.

He kept his eyes open as Hester continued their tour of the village, package holding the bonnet swinging from one hand. Bascom already carried packages Elizabeth had purchased from Mr. Carroll, though Rob had convinced her to leave the hippopotamus in its corner.

All the Colors of the Sea, across the street from Mr. Carroll's Curiosities, offered handcrafts from local families along with a stunning set of paintings by the physician's wife, Mrs. Abigail Bennett. Hester took a moment to speak to the lady privately, then lingered over the landscapes, until he was highly tempted to buy her one. If only he could convince himself it wouldn't cause a scandal.

But the earl hardly needed paintings either.

The village boasted a tailor, a barber, and a jeweler as well as a shop that specialized in ladies' bonnets. His sister purchased a carnelian ring from Mr. Lawrence, the jeweler, and a flowered hat from Mrs. Rinehart, the milliner. Elizabeth also insisted on visiting the linens and trimmings shop, where two older ladies, sisters by the looks of them, fawned over her. His sister fingered the goods with longing and came away with some ribbons and a length of Merino wool the color of plums, which only added to the teetering pile in Bascom's slender arms. Still, Rob saw nothing that might interest Lord Howland or his bride.

Hester kept glancing at him, and he couldn't tell if she thought him too fastidious in his choices or wondered whether he simply didn't care.

"Did nothing pique your interest?" she asked as they neared the harbor, where fishing boats bobbed at anchor alongside a few pleasure craft.

Elizabeth turned her gaze from the view, lips downturned, and he knew she must be thinking of the ill-fated boat that had sank under their parents.

"Not yet," Rob told Hester. "Tell me, what have you heard about the earl's current situation, his reason for residing in Grace-by-the-Sea."

Her gaze went out over the waves as well. "It is not spoken of in public, but I understand the previous earl's death may have caused some financial constraints. The current earl is working hard to rectify them."

Which meant that economies were being made. The dowager countess wouldn't like that. Neither would Howland's daughter.

Just then Rob's gaze lit on one of the shops closest to the harbor, and inspiration struck.

"Ellison's Bakery," he said, eyeing the sign over the half door. "I seem to recall Father praising its wares."

"Wasn't it cinnamon buns?" Elizabeth asked, fond smile reappearing.

"Mr. Ellison is rather famous for them," Hester acknowledged.

"And is there something in particular your sister or Lady Miranda favors?" Rob asked her.

"Rosemary has mentioned a particular bread with caraway seeds," she said, frown gathering as if she wasn't sure why he had asked.

"I'll take that as a recommendation." Rob headed for the door. "Give me a few moments, then I'll join you. Bascom, stay with the ladies."

Mr. Ellison, a broad fellow who could as easily have been the village blacksmith, readily agreed to Rob's plan. And he added six of his succulent cinnamon buns for Rob to take home.

As they started up the street for the carriage, Elizabeth lagged behind with Bascom, sniffing deeply, as if she would inhale the buns in the box he carried.

"I know you'll enjoy those," Hester said beside Rob, "but it's a shame you didn't find a gift to your liking."

He could leave her with that impression, perhaps inveigle another trip for the purpose of finding a present, but he could not bring himself to lie to her again. "Actually, I found just what I was seeking. It's unconventional, but then, so am I."

Hester glanced his way again. "Do I dare ask what you've done?"

Rob smiled. "Thanks to your recommendation, Mr. Ellison will be delivering fresh bread and sweet treats to the castle for the next year on behalf of the Peverells."

She stopped, forcing him up as well. Elizabeth nearly collided with them before catching herself. Even Bascom stumbled, juggling the packages to keep them from dropping.

Hester's blue-green eyes were shining, like sunlight reflecting off the waters of the cove. "Rob, that is beyond kind. It will mean so much to Rosemary, Lady Miranda, and the earl. It's a clever gift that helps without shaming them for their current situation. Thank you."

Was that heat in his cheeks? He couldn't remember the last time he'd blushed. "I would hope for the same kindness should I be in a situation not of my making."

She nodded thoughtfully. "I'll remember that."

Elizabeth pushed past him with an arch look. "So will I." She lowered her voice as Hester started forward. "Because the last time I checked, Brother, you are in a situation not of your own making. Have some patience with yourself."

Perhaps when he'd grown into his role. He might not have inherited Howland's financial troubles, but he had a long way to go to fill his father's place.

Hester kept glancing at Rob as the coach carried them

back toward Upper Grace. He sat beside her, swaying with the coach's movement, his broad shoulder bumping hers, his trousers brushing her skirts. She knew when he sighed and when his gaze dropped to his gloved hands on his thighs. When he aimed his smile at her, her heart felt the hit.

Yet, who was he? The man she'd known seven years ago would not have thought of that kind gesture of delivering bread to a family too proud to admit openly it was in need. Was it possible he truly had changed?

She roused herself as they came into Upper Grace and had him direct his coachman around the back of the house after they had alighted, where her family coachman would help him see to the horses and provide some refreshment. She sent young Ike Bascom, who was apparently acting as footman during Rob and Elizabeth's visit, to the kitchen for refreshment as well before escorting her guests into the sitting room.

Her mother rose from the sofa to greet them. "Lord Peverell, Miss Peverell, you honor us."

"On the contrary," Elizabeth said, moving to join her. "You honor us by your invitation. You are the very first to think of including us."

"Well," her mother said, turning a pleased pink, "I certainly won't be the last. Please, have a seat. Tea should be here shortly."

Elizabeth sat on the sofa beside Hester's mother, but Rob could not seem to decide where to land. He moved from the wood-wrapped hearth to the curtained window and back to the sofa.

A clatter on the stairs warned Hester a moment before Rebecca burst into the room. "Mama!"

She caught her as her daughter careened into her. "Rebecca, we have company. Please greet Lord Peverell and his sister."

Her daughter turned dutifully, though she pressed herself back into Hester's skirts. "Thank you for coming to see us, Lord Peverell, Miss Peverell. I hope you are well."

Rob came around the sofa to smile at her. "Quite well. And you?"

"Tolerable," Rebecca allowed, and Hester had to hide a grin at the big word.

As her mother smiled, Elizabeth edged over and patted the sofa beside her. "Why don't you sit by me, Miss Todd, while we wait for tea?"

"She called me Miss Todd," Rebecca whispered with a giggle to Hester.

"And you should answer her," Hester reminded her.

Rebecca raised her chin and minced across the room to push herself up onto the sofa. "Don't mind if I do, Miss Peverell."

The housemaid came in then with a plate of biscuits. She must have enlisted Ike's help, for he carried a tray with the tea and cups. Her mother began dispensing the brew. Rob finally consented to sit near Hester on one of the armchairs.

"Did you enjoy the shops, Miss Peverell?" her mother asked as the plate of biscuits began making its rounds. Rebecca watched the progress, and Hester watched Rebecca.

"They were delightful," Elizabeth said. "Do you have a favorite?"

"All the Colors of the Sea," her mother admitted. "I'm very fond of the tatted collars." She fingered the knot-work at her neck as if to prove it.

Oh, but Hester knew where this was going. Before she could think of a way to steer the conversation in another direction, Elizabeth took the bait.

"Oh, that is lovely. A local tatter, I take it?"

"Indeed," her mother said with a proud smile. "Hester makes them to raise money for the dame school."

"Does she indeed?" Now Rob's smile was nearly as

proud.

"I do," Hester told him defensively.

Elizabeth leaned closer to Rebecca. "Perhaps you and your grandmother could help me decide what type of collar would look best on me."

"A pink one," Rebecca said. "I like pink."

"So do I," Elizabeth assured her, and all at once the three of them had their heads together.

Colluding again.

Hester cast Rob an apologetic smile, and he winked at her. She made herself sip her tea. Why was she finding it so difficult to spend a moment alone with him? She had once enjoyed listening to him. He could spin a tale better than anyone, until you were certain he believed it too. If he ever grew as fanciful as Aunt Maudie, they were all in trouble.

"What are your plans for the future?" she asked, hoping to get him started.

He stretched out his long legs until his toes brushed hers. "Elizabeth and I will be here for a time, as she noted to you. I thought the quiet here would do us good."

"It is quiet," Hester agreed. "But I was under the impression you didn't like quiet."

He studied the toe of his boot as it swung against her skirts. "I have come to value it, in the right amounts." He shot her a grin. "Not that I'm opposed to excitement, mind you."

Now, that was the Rob she knew. "And what excites you now?"

"You."

She sloshed the tea and just managed to level the cup before she spilled on her gown. She could not look at him.

"You should not say such things to me," she whispered, mindful of her mother, Elizabeth, and Rebecca across the room. "I won't be your entertainment this time."

His foot withdrew. "No, of course not. Forgive me. That wasn't what I meant. Your company has brightened a time when Elizabeth and I struggle to find our way out of the darkness. I had hope the three of us might be friends. I could use a friend now."

She chanced a glance at him and found his head down, hair curling toward his cheek. He looked so sad, so lost.

"In truth, I could use a friend as well," she said.

"Friends, then," he replied, but she was certain she heard the words *for now*.

CHAPTER EIGHT

ROB COULD ONLY BE PLEASED as he and Elizabeth headed for home at last. Not only had he helped his fellow landowner, and the local shops, but Hester was warming to him. He could see it in the way her eyes softened when she looked at him, hear it in the approval in her voice. Friends, she'd said, with a gentle smile that made him hope for more. Perhaps he had a chance of rekindling their relationship.

He frowned as the coach headed for the Lodge. Wasn't he doing all this from a desire to atone, to prove to himself he was a changed man? When had atonement become hope? He wasn't sure his father would have approved of Hester as the wife of his second son. Others would be sure to question her appropriateness for the bride of a viscount. If he pursued her, would he be subjecting her to criticism?

"You're rather Friday-faced after such a pleasant afternoon," Elizabeth said from across the coach. "I thought you and Hester were getting on well."

"Quite well," Rob agreed, turning to face his sister. "But then, we always did."

"And that gives you such a prodigious frown?"

Rob chuckled. "I wasn't aware I was capable of prodigious frowns."

"I wish I had a mirror. It is quite prodigious."

He made a show of wiggling his brows, his nose, and his mouth all at once. "Better?"

Elizabeth laughed. "No! You've only made it worse."

"Well, then, I suppose I should be glad you're the only one to see it."

Her look dimmed. "I can think of three others who would have enjoyed it as much."

So could he. "They will always be with us, Elizabeth. But they would want us to be happy."

She sighed. "I know. And I'm trying. Truly. All seems bright and good, and then I remember."

He reached across and held her hand a moment. "I know. But I am told it will get better with time."

She nodded and gave him a shadow of a smile.

He did not see a smile again until Mr. Donner came calling late Monday morning, putting Rob in the position of playing chaperone.

It was the oddest feeling, being in their mother's favorite withdrawing room overlooking the Channel while Donner and Elizabeth sat on the striped sofa and made polite conversation. His presence had usually been the cause of a lady needing a chaperone. And Mother normally played that role with Elizabeth.

He could feel her presence even now. She'd had the room redecorated in pale greens and warm rose, and he almost fancied he could catch a glimpse of her reflection in the massive, gilt-framed mirror over the white marble hearth.

"Perhaps, if the weather holds, we might take a drive along the coast road," Donner was suggesting now. The tight set to his shoulders and the way his feet shifted on the leafy pattern of the Aubusson carpet said how badly he wanted Rob's sister to agree.

"I think that would be lovely, Mr. Donner," she replied, gaze on her hands, folded in the lap of her grey poplin gown.

Donner's grin lit the room. "I'll enquire of Mr. Josephs at the livery stable about a gig."

Rob stirred himself. "Perhaps something a bit larger. So there's room for Elizabeth's maid."

Elizabeth shot him a dark look before smiling at Donner. "Or my brother. Rob loves riding in carriages."

Wretch. She knew he far preferred horseback. Thomas had never let Rob forget the two times he'd ridden in the backward-facing seat on the way to their country house in Wiltshire and they had had to stop the coach so Rob could be sick.

"Yes, yes, of course," Donner said. "I intended to invite you to join us, my lord."

Of course he had.

Rob settled in the high-backed upholstered chair, trying not to drum his fingers on the dark-wood arms, and watched Elizabeth and her would-be swain discuss inanities as if they feared delving into anything of substance would shackle themselves to each other. Did he and Hester look like that now? What he wouldn't give for the camaraderie they'd once shared. They could laugh easily, talk readily. Well, about everything except their true identities. Was this cautious stiffness any better?

Donner stood and bowed over Elizabeth's hand, and Rob realized the fellow was taking his leave. As Rob stood too, Donner looked his way, face once more tight.

"Might I have a private word, my lord, before I go?"

Behind Donner's back, Elizabeth shook her head hard. Rob had the same thought. The fellow could not be asking for the right to propose so soon. He'd spoken to Elizabeth no more than three times since being introduced. What, was he a fortune hunter?

That frown his sister called prodigious must have appeared on his face, for Donner paled.

"Certainly, sir," Rob said. "Elizabeth, if you would leave us a moment."

His sister rose and gave Donner a polite smile before crossing in front of him. Her gaze met Rob's, pointed. She needn't have worried. He had no intention of turning her over to a stranger. Few were in his father's league for dispensing stern words to suitors, but Rob would do what he must to protect his sister.

Donner followed her to the door, then shut it, and Rob tensed further.

"Is there some need for secrecy, sir?" he demanded as Donner passed him again.

He thought the fellow would resume his seat on the sofa, but the bounder had the audacity to move to the window and draw the drapes!

"Forgive me, my lord," he said, as if that could erase the high-handed offense. "But I will take no chances that our conversation is seen or overheard."

Rob raised a brow as Donner turned to face him. "Is there some reason your pursuit of my sister must be a state secret?" he asked.

Donner flamed. "I am not pursuing your sister. That is," he hurried on when Rob narrowed his eyes at him, "I would be beyond delighted if your sister were to return half the admiration I feel for her. But my purpose in calling today was for a moment of your time."

Rob crossed his arms over his chest. "Why?"

Donner reached into his dove grey morning coat, removed a folded piece of parchment, and held it out to him. "I am an agent of the War Office, sent to Grace-by-the-Sea to ferret out a smuggling ring connected to our enemies in France."

Rob accepted the parchment and gave it a quick read. The letter from the War Office seemed official, down to its Royal seal and lordly signature, but such things could have been fabricated.

"Will the Earl of Howland and Mr. Howland, the magistrate, vouch for you?" Rob asked him, handing back the letter.

Donner shook his head as he accepted it. "No. Neither knows my true purpose. I was advised not to trust either of them, nor the Riding Surveyor, Mr. Denby."

Denby? That must be Hester's brother. Rob couldn't help his chuckle. "And you were advised to trust *me*? I fear for the war effort."

The so-called agent frowned. "Your father and brother were staunch supporters of Mr. Pitt and the King."

"They certainly were," Rob agreed. "But I have more in common with our charming Heir Apparent than his father."

Donner's frown only grew. "Then you refuse to help?"

"I didn't say that." Rob sat and nodded Donner back onto the sofa. "I am Viscount Peverell now. Of course I will do my duty. I'm merely surprised that you doubt the same would be said of the Howlands or Mr. Denby."

Donner leaned back on the sofa. "I'm more saddened than surprised. Mr. Denby has done well enough surveying the area, but the incidents continue. We have evidence to suggest that the previous Earl of Howland actively supported local smugglers known to have ties to France. We therefore cannot be certain of his son. And there have been too many oddities in recent months for me to feel comfortable enlisting the aid of the magistrate."

"Oddities?" Rob pressed. "Such as?"

Donner rubbed a hand along his breeches. "Recently, Doctor Bennett and his wife captured a French agent masquerading as a visiting physician at the spa."

"Doctor Bennett captured the fellow?" Rob interrupted. "On your orders?"

Donner colored. "Not exactly. I had suspected there were spies about, but Owens was a master of disguise."

Not so much a master that the amateur physician and his wife had mistaken him, but Rob decided not to rub salt in the agent's wound.

"We also had a scare when a ship flying French colors sailed into the annual regatta in August and prompted an evacuation," Donner continued undaunted. "Your steward will have alerted you that most of the village used your house as shelter."

Funny that Mercer hadn't seen fit to mention that. Rob inclined his head but promised himself he would ask his steward about the matter.

"And," Donner added, "before I arrived, we were advised that a French sympathizer had been caught intercepting notes passed by a mysterious fellow calling himself the Lord of the Smugglers. He apparently had access to Castle How when it was empty."

Rob stiffened. "Did you hear of such things happening here at the Lodge?"

"Not notes," Donner assured him. "We have no reason to believe your home is in danger. We are more interested in the pier below the Lodge."

"We've had the same concerns," Rob told him. "Elizabeth and I saw a blue flash the other night, as if smugglers were attempting to come in. I sent word to my steward to hire a night watchman, but I have not been informed of anyone on the grounds or the pier."

Donner leaned forward. "Yet. I have no doubt your pier will prove too tempting. Until now, the caves beneath Castle How on the other headland have been the focus of all activity. When Miss Denby discovered her crocodile on the cliffs near the cave's entrance from the sea, she doomed that area to interest from visitors. Now there are too many people about to make it a safe landing area, whatever time of day."

"The Dragon's Maw," Rob remembered. "I've heard the old stories. The opening can only be navigated at the turn of the tide and could keep a ship stranded until the tide turns again."

"Making your pier entirely too useful to forego, particularly by this so-called Lord of the Smugglers," Donner told him. "We have reason to believe more than lace and champagne comes in with his shipments, and he carries our secrets to France. I expect he may contact you, request the use of your pier, perhaps your cellars to store his ill-gotten goods until he can safely move them inland. A dram for the lord, you know."

Once he would have jumped at the chance. Duty-free champagne and fine Alençon lace for allowing the use of his facilities? What a bargain. What an adventure.

"What do you want from me?" Rob asked, watching Donner.

The fellow's grey eyes kindled. "When the smugglers approach you, agree to as much as you feel comfortable and learn all that you can. Then, tell me, and, I promise you, the War Office will pounce and stop this fiend once and for all."

It was dangerous. Donner had obviously failed in the past. Rob might not be able to count on the War Office to do its part.

But lack of support for his audacious deeds—whether his father or the government—had never stopped him before.

He snapped a nod. "Count on me, Mr. Donner. But do not involve my sister further. She's been through a great deal recently. I will not have her heart broken by a fictitious romance."

Donner colored once more. Truly, the fellow had no ability for subterfuge. "I assure you my intentions toward your sister are honorable. I would be the most fortunate man alive to be allowed to pay my respects. But I am aware of the gulf between our stations."

"Good," Rob said, for all he didn't care about that gulf. "See that you remember that and treat her accordingly. Now, how do you suggest I go about making the acquaintance of the Lord of the Smugglers?"

Hester could only be glad that Monday was to be a blur of activity. She must teach at the school, then rush home to help her mother with preparations for Rosemary's wedding on Thursday. Surely all that would keep her mind off Rob.

It didn't.

She thought of him as she and Rebecca trudged to the school through the crisp autumn morning. Because of his generosity, they would soon have a hearth to warm the building. One less excuse for her more-reluctant students to stay away. One more reason to be thankful.

After school, she and Rebecca went to try on their new dresses. The seamstress in Upper Grace had used her and Rebecca's previous measurements to create new gowns for the wedding, as Hester and her daughter were to be Rosemary's attendants. Her mother also had a new gown.

"I'm sure there will be a few tucks needed," she fussed as the seamstress moved around her, eyeing the purple material.

"Or perhaps a seam or hem let out," Hester said with a smile at her daughter.

Rebecca wiggled a little as she regarded herself in the Pier glass mirror in the corner of the shop.

"I look pretty," she said.

"You always look pretty," Hester assured her, "but that rosy color does favor you."

Rebecca swished the silky skirt from side to side. "Can we make one for Esmeralda too?"

Hester glanced to the wooden doll regarding them with its painted eyes from a chair across the room. She'd allowed Rebecca to bring it to keep herself entertained, if needed.

"The fabric is too dear," she explained to her daughter, "but I'll see if we have anything this color in the trimmings bag at home."

"I wish I could take her to the wedding," Rebecca said with a look to Hester as the seamstress began to pin up her mother's hem.

"You will be far too busy at the wedding to play with Esmeralda," Hester told her, starting to unfasten the back of the gown before her daughter could wrinkle it. "But you can tell her all about it when you get home."

"But I want her to meet Lord Peverell," Rebecca protested, raising her arms so Hester could slip the gown off over her head. "I didn't get a chance to introduce her when he was here for tea."

Hester glanced to her mother and the seamstress, but they appeared engaged in their discussion about the perfect length of a gown for dancing.

"Lord Peverell will likely be too busy as well," Hester told her, laying the dress safely aside.

"Next time he comes for tea?" Rebecca asked plaintively.

How could she promise her daughter Rob would return? She wasn't sure when she might see him again. Unlike second sons, viscounts did not have the luxury of strolling the Downs looking for pretty girls to woo.

"Perhaps," Hester said, rising from where she'd knelt beside her daughter.

Her mother bustled up to them and turned this way and that. "What do you think? Is the color too bold for a woman of my years?"

Hester regarded the deep purple, like mulberries. "Not at all, Mother. You look very well in it."

She plucked at the gentle dip of the neckline. "Perhaps a bit of lace?"

"If it pleases you." Hester held out her hands as the

seamstress brought her dress. Such a fine silk, such a pretty color. Rebecca wasn't the only one who looked good in rose.

"You should not wear lace," her mother said as Hester took the dress. "I want you looking your best too. Men think about marriage at weddings."

Her cheeks were probably as rosy as her gown. She tipped her head to where Rebecca was smoothing down Esmeralda's skirts and promising the doll she would have a new gown soon. "Please, Mother. Let's not go into that here."

Her mother frowned as the seamstress began unfastening Hester's dress so she could try on the new gown. "Why not? You have every right to think about marrying again."

"So I can have a father," Rebecca piped up.

The seamstress's brows rose, and Hester pinned her mother with a look and a shake of her head. She managed to keep them off the subject of marriages and fathers until they had finished at the shop, returned home, and sent Rebecca up to the nursery.

But her mother obviously had more to say about the matter.

"Rosemary is marrying an earl," she reminded Hester as they retired to the sitting room. "I see no reason why you shouldn't marry a viscount."

Hester's hands were shaking as she went to a chair. "Because he doesn't want me, Mother."

Her mother sniffed. "Not from what I can see. He's been very kind and generous to you and yours—the school, your sister. He's sat through tea with Rebecca. A viscount doesn't do that sort of thing unless he's interested."

She still couldn't convince herself, but she couldn't explain to her mother her past with Rob and why he might want to atone for it.

But did his attentions stem from a desire to atone? She could not make up her mind after her mother had gone to fetch the sewing box. The Rob she'd known had only apologized if it benefitted him in some way, and then he would turn the apology into some clever joke. She could not see how donating to the school or helping Rosemary benefitted him. What was he after?

On the other hand, she wasn't sure what she was after, encouraging him. Once she'd been as big a dreamer as Rob—thinking about a future where she and her beloved husband had a big house, filled with happy children. She'd receive the finest ladies in the village, her good taste so well regarded that she would be asked to advise on fashion and furnishings. She'd contribute to her congregation and her community.

Only the last had come true, and more from Rosemary's doing than hers. After Rob had left, everything had changed so fast—wife, mother, widow—that she'd never entirely found her footing again.

And she'd stopped dreaming.

Odd to realize that now. When was the last time she'd thought of the future without trepidation? Her sister had sought to step out on her own as a governess, and Hester had worried. The earl had shown an interest in Rosemary, and Hester had tried to set him straight. She couldn't bear for her sister to be hurt the way she had been.

But it had all come right. Rosemary had made a marvelous governess. The earl had asked for her hand in marriage. They both seemed deliriously happy.

Perhaps it was time to dust off her own dreams again.

CHAPTER NINE

"THE CARRIAGE IS READY, MY lord," Bascom announced Tuesday late morning as he stood in the doorway of the withdrawing room Rob's mother had favored.

As Rob turned away from the view out over the Channel, Elizabeth frowned.

"The carriage?" she asked, setting aside her embroidery. "Are we visiting today?"

Rob reached for the black stock around his neck, then dropped his fingers before he could dislodge it. "I had a matter I wished to discuss with Hester."

Donner hadn't had much advice about making connections with the smugglers, but it had struck him that, as the teacher at the dame school, Hester probably spoke with the very people most likely to be involved. While the aristocrats and gentry enjoyed the duty-free goods that appeared as if by magic on their back stoops, the farmers, laborers, and merchants would be the ones arranging for and carrying those goods about the area. One likely acted as lander, who organized the signal for the ships to come in and teams to ferry their plunder inland.

Elizabeth stood to intercept him as he started across the room. "A matter? About what, precisely?"

He hadn't been given leave to share Donner's story from the day before, though he'd certainly thought about it more than once since.

"Rumors have come my way," he hedged. "I thought she might know something of them."

Elizabeth rolled her eyes. "I will not be shut out of such an intriguing conversation. Bascom, ask Kinsey to fetch me my grey velvet hat and the grey redingote. I will accompany my brother."

Rob tried not to sigh.

Truly, he would not have been able to speak with Hester alone in any event. Her mother and daughter would likely be in attendance as well. But having Elizabeth along meant he'd have to be even more careful in how he phrased his questions.

The morning had been challenging enough. Mercer had arrived with additional papers to sign. Rob had dutifully reviewed each and affixed his signature.

"And were there any repercussions concerning the house after the village evacuated here in August?" he asked as he handed his steward the last piece of parchment.

Mercer regarded Rob as if he had barked like a dog instead of asking a perfectly reasonable question. "Mrs. Kirby, the leasing agent, informed me that Mrs. Catchpole dispatched a cleaning crew," his steward answered. "Have you found something amiss?"

"Only that I wasn't told of the incident," Rob pointed out.

Mercer had the good sense to drop his gaze to the portfolio sticking out from under his slender arm. "You and Miss Peverell were still discussing where you would finish your mourning period, my lord. I didn't wish to intrude with news that could in no way influence that decision."

"Kind of you," Rob acknowledged. "In the future, however, I'd like to know everything about my holdings, no matter how trivial."

Mercer nodded. "Then I will tell you that we have some concerns about the stability of the rear wing. You and Miss Peverell had not planned to use it, so I saw no reason to mention the matter. But, since you ask…"

The rear wing, one of the most recent additions to his sprawling lodge, stuck out from the southwest corner of the building at a forty-five-degree angle pointing toward the boating shed. It housed a ballroom, receiving rooms, and other function spaces as well as bedchambers for guests on the upper floors.

"What sort of concerns?" Rob asked.

Mercer grimaced. "The foundation may not have been fixed properly. I'll consult an architect once you and Miss Peverell are safety returned to London. Will there be anything else, my lord?"

Surprising how his steward was less patient than Rob. "Yes. You were to hire a night watchman. I've heard nothing further."

Mercer drew himself up. "I assure you that I have done as you asked, my lord. Mr. Chalder, a respected local fellow, will come in from dusk to dawn to watch over the property. You won't even notice he's around."

"Excellent," Rob said. "I'd like him to report to me every morning before leaving."

Mercer started. "That could be quite early, my lord."

Rob smiled. "I've been rising remarkably early of late. It will be no trouble."

Mercer's smile was strained. "Very well, my lord, if you think it necessary."

"I'll expect to see him first thing tomorrow," Rob told him.

Mercer had hugged his portfolio closer and bowed himself out.

After such an encounter, Rob was heartily glad he was going to seek someone of a more congenial nature, like Hester. Her mother, in particular, seemed delighted to receive him and Elizabeth, seeing them settled in the sitting room while a maid went to inform Hester and her daughter of their arrival.

Rebecca came hugging a wooden doll, the bonnet Hester had purchased on Saturday covering most of the toy's painted flaxen curls. Rob stood as Hester and her daughter dropped curtsies.

"Lord Peverell, Elizabeth," Hester said in her quiet voice. "How nice to see you."

"Hester," he said, savoring her first name. "Miss Todd. And, unless I miss my guess, this is Esmeralda."

Rebecca clutched the doll closer. "How did you know?"

"Your mother told me about your special friend," Rob told her.

Rebecca glanced down at the doll. "She is very pleased to make your acquaintance."

Rob bowed. "And I am pleased to make hers."

One hand on her daughter's shoulder, Hester guided her to a seat near the hearth. Rob stationed himself close by, as Mrs. Denby and Elizabeth took the sofa.

"We'll have lemonade shortly," she announced before looking to his sister. "And how have you been enjoying yourself, Miss Peverell?"

"I've been reading some of the novels in our library here," his sister confessed. "There's one in particular I'd like your opinion on, but there's no need to bother Rob and Hester about the matter. We'll just put our heads together." The two suited word to action.

Hester looked to Rob. "Colluding," she whispered.

"Indeed," he agreed, enjoying the way the light from the fire brought out the gold in her hair.

"What's colluding?" Rebecca whispered, glancing between them.

Hester blushed.

"When two or more people share a secret from others,"

Rob answered for her. "Your mother and I have a feeling your grandmother and my sister are sharing a secret even now. Perhaps you'd like to go listen."

Rebecca nodded, deposited Esmeralda on her chair, and ventured closer to the pair on the sofa.

"You shouldn't encourage her," Hester told him. "She overhears entirely too much as it is."

"It's only for a moment," he promised her. "I've been given some disturbing news, and I was hoping you could help me ferret out the truth."

Immediately she was all attention. "What's happened?"

"I have been informed that a ship is docking at my pier on dark nights. My steward and I suspect smugglers."

She shuddered, color leaching from her cheeks. "I certainly hope not. Lark, my brother, and his local Riding Officer, Alexander Chance, do their best to make sure we aren't troubled by such criminals. And Abigail told me Saturday that the French spies have been chased out of the area."

"French spies?"

He must have raised his voice, for both her mother and Elizabeth glanced his way. Rebecca frowned, as if she expected better of him.

He gave them his best smile.

"Forgive me," he murmured to Hester. "You took me by surprise. How did you and Abigail know there were French spies in the area?"

"Stories abound," she said. "The two most recent fellows frequented the spa, hiding among the visitors. To think I actually danced with them!" She shuddered again.

"Amazing," he said. "The spa seems in all ways benevolent."

"It is," Hester said. "As is Grace-by-the-Sea and Upper Grace. But we have found it important to defend ourselves. The magistrate leads a Men's Militia. Abigail Bennett and Jesslyn chartered one for the women."

He started. "Grace-by-the-Sea has a Women's Militia? Don't tell Elizabeth. She'll want to join."

"She would be most welcome," Hester told him. "And needed. We have seen more than our share of spies and smugglers ever since Napoleon started gathering his troops across the Channel. Some people claim they hide in abandoned homes: farmsteads left for the winter, the Castle, the Lodge."

That set his skin to crawling. "I wish I could assure you no one was hiding in the Lodge, but we haven't opened half the rooms. A French battalion could have taken up residence, and I wouldn't know it until they came to demand breakfast from our chef. Tell me, have you heard stories about a Lord of the Smugglers as well?"

She nodded. "Jesslyn and the villagers routed him months ago. He and his gang were taken into custody."

Was that what the magistrate had meant when Rob had talked to him earlier? "You're certain?" Rob pressed her.

"Absolutely," she said. "It was in the *Upper Grace Gazette*, and Mr. Peascoate is very careful to confirm all stories before printing. Besides, Lark was more than delighted to regale us with the tale. He hadn't been made Riding Surveyor yet, but he was involved in Mr. Bascom's capture."

Rob blinked. "Bascom? Any relation to my footman?"

"His father," she said. "And I must say it was very kind of you to hire young Ike. He hasn't had an easy go of it, I understand."

He hadn't hired the fellow. Elizabeth had, and he was certain she'd had no knowledge of the boy's background. Yet he could not believe it a coincidence that the son of smugglers had started working at the Lodge just as a gang of smugglers thought to make use of it.

Did Donner know about Bascom's father? For that matter, why was Donner claiming the Lord of the Smugglers still active when he'd been captured months ago?

Surely the War Office wasn't *that* far behind.

Either the intelligence agent was lying, or Grace-by-the-Sea and the Lodge were in more danger than the villagers knew.

Rob nodded to Hester's praise, but his lovely hazel eyes had gone unfocused, as if his mind raced ahead to something else. He did not comment further, turning instead to inquire after her mother's health and Rebecca's progress in school. He and Elizabeth drank the lemonade the maid served, then took their leave, as polite as any other acquaintances. He had come for answers, and she had given them. As simple as that.

But the visit only raised expectations.

"So nice of them to call," her mother enthused.

"He liked Esmeralda," Rebecca said as if she were a proud mama.

"He liked your mother too," her grandmother said with a look to Hester.

Hester wasn't so sure. With his questions about smugglers and spies, it still seemed a bit as if Rob had sought her out for entertainment.

But Rob was certainly the entertainment at the assembly Wednesday evening.

It was quieter than usual, mostly the members of the Spa Corporation Council and their families along with the Regulars and a few Newcomers to the spa. Her brother Lark had returned from his sweep down the coast as well. He didn't have much of an opportunity to speak to her, because her mother, Jesslyn, and Rosemary kept grouping and regrouping to discuss the preparations for the wedding tomorrow. Hester's sister had been living with Lark and Jesslyn since the announcement of her betrothal, but she intended to sleep in her old room in Upper Grace one last time tonight. Rebecca had been given permission to stay up and visit.

The attention to Rob quite eclipsed the upcoming nuptials. The vicar followed him about with puppy-like adoration, Mr. and Mrs. Greer cornered him, and Mr. Donner clung to his side so tightly Hester's former devoted dance partner didn't even take the opportunity to ask her out on the floor. She wasn't entirely surprised when Rob threw them all off, face hinting of desperation, and retreated to her side.

"Smile," he instructed her as he sank onto the chair beside her. "Pretend you are delighted to see me."

"Why do you need my delight?" Hester asked, though she did smile. "You appear to be the talk of the village tonight."

He tugged at his cravat around his neck. "I'm entirely too popular. One more conversation with the vicar, and I'll likely donate the Lodge for the care and feeding of indigent pigeons."

Hester laughed, then schooled her face as Mrs. Greer ventured closer.

"My lord," she said, completely ignoring Hester at his side. "We were wondering. That is, I had thought. Well, what would you think about an appointment to the spa council?"

She obviously considered it a boon. Her beaming smile said as much. Hester glanced at Rob. It was such a tiny thing compared to the title and privileges he now wielded. Would he understand?

He stood and took the lady's hand, then bowed over it. "You honor me, Mrs. Greer. But I cannot know when I will be called back to London about some matter of import to the nation. Perhaps you might consider Lord Featherstone as my agent. I have found him to be of sound mind and civil demeanor."

"An excellent suggestion, my lord," she simpered as he released her. "I'll go ask him this very moment and let you know his answer." She turned in a swirl of white silk and hurried off.

"Quick," Rob said, holding out a hand to Hester. "Have pity and dance with me. Please."

She could not refuse such a request. She took his hand and let him lead her onto the floor.

They had never danced in public before. On one occasion, she remembered, he'd capered across the grass while they both laughed, but that was as close as they had come. She wasn't surprised to find him graceful and accomplished. Indeed, he excelled in the little extra flourishes—skipping when he might have walked, pointing his toe when others merely took a step. The looks being directed her way from some of the other ladies could only be called envious.

And when he took her hands and twirled her, her heart danced as well.

Perhaps she should have refused to partner him. She'd only raised her mother's expectations anew, and after this, half of Upper Grace would be gossiping as well. Yet dancing with Rob felt so good, so free, that she allowed herself a moment to forget her concerns, lost in the joy of simply being with him.

The relatively few dancers meant they must stand out for a measure at one point. Hester became aware of Mrs. Greer pacing along the edge of the dancefloor, as if ready to pounce on Rob the moment the music stopped.

"Why did you refuse her?" Hester asked. "I don't recall your father having a post of great import in the government."

He kept his face toward her, but she could see his gaze following the Spa Corporation Council president's wife. "In truth, I didn't think it my place. Who am I to say what Grace-by-the-Sea's famous spa should be?"

Hester stared at him. "Who are *you*? You are Viscount Peverell, owner of most of the property in the area."

He tugged at his cravat again, wrinkling the material beyond redemption. "That is what I try to tell myself."

She could not believe his humility. "What happened to that brash young man who pretended to court me one summer?"

He met her gaze, his own dark and determined. "He became a more solid fellow who no longer has the luxury of pretending."

The music required their attention then, and she did not have an opportunity to question him further. He only had a moment to return her to her chair before Mrs. Greer captured him and dragged him off on some errand. Hester watched as he consulted with Lord Featherstone and Mr. Greer, Mr. Donner hovering nearby. It was all very civil and proper. The sort of steady fellow she applauded.

What was she to do with the new Rob?

CHAPTER TEN

S HE DID NOT HAVE ANOTHER opportunity to speak to Rob before her mother and Rosemary collected her to return home. For a moment, in the coach, it was like yesterday—the three of them united, making plans, strategizing actions. But as the coach approached Upper Grace, their mother directed her attention to Hester.

"Lord Peverell was quite solicitous," she ventured. "Even if Mrs. Greer saw fit to monopolize his time."

Rosemary cast Hester a quick glance. "She must toady while she can, Mother. He'll likely be leaving soon."

The fact was not as encouraging as it once had been.

As soon as they returned to the house, they all retreated to the room Hester and Rosemary had once shared, where Rebecca waited, stockinged feet sticking out below her pink flannel nightgown and arms hugging Esmeralda, who was also dressed for bed in a matching nightgown. Hester sat on the bed and tucked her daughter close as her mother and sister examined the new gowns, which had been delivered that afternoon.

Their mother alternated between beaming and bawling, though she insisted they were tears of joy.

"At least one of my daughters will be happily wed," she explained, dabbing at her eyes as if fearing her tears would fall on the fine silk.

"Hester was happily wed, too, Mother," Rosemary reminded her with a look to Rebecca, who was watching her grandmother with obvious concern.

"Of course she was," their mother agreed with a sniff. "But we all know what happened to Lieutenant Todd."

"My papa was a hero," Rebecca chimed in, hugging Esmeralda. "He was very brave. I must be very brave too."

Hester slipped an arm about her daughter's shoulders where she sat next to her on the bed. "Right now, let's just be happy for your aunt Rosemary. You remember your part in the wedding?"

Rebecca nodded solemnly. "I carry a basket of pretty leaves in front of Aunt Rosemary all the way to the vicar. And I walk like a lady, no running or skipping."

"Very good," Rosemary said. "And then where do you go?"

"To Grandmother," Rebecca said.

"That's right," Hester told her. "I'll be walking right behind you, but I'll need to stay at the altar with Aunt Rosemary. You'll sit with your grandmother in the very front pew on the side opposite the pretty glass windows."

"Oh, it will be so lovely," their mother said, tears starting to flow again.

"Now, Mother," Rosemary said, wrapping her arms around her. "Why don't you get some rest? I'm sure Rebecca would love to have you tuck her in too."

Rebecca looked up at Hester. "Must I go? I want to stay with you and Aunt Rosemary."

Hester kissed the top of her head. "It's already far past your bedtime, and tomorrow will be a busy day. Go with your grandmother now."

With a sigh, her daughter suffered to slip from the bed and pad beside Hester's mother from the room.

Rosemary came to sit on the bed next to Hester. "Hurry, before the maid comes to help us change. Why are you encouraging Lord Peverell?"

Hester's fingers knit into the soft materials of her ball-gown. "I haven't been encouraging him, but I cannot find it in me to completely discourage him, either."

Rosemary sighed. "You are one of the gentlest souls I know, Hester, but there is a time for standing your ground. You know him to be a scoundrel. Send him packing."

Hester glanced up at her with a frown. "Is it not possible that he has changed? And if he has, shouldn't he be given the opportunity to prove as much?"

"No," Rosemary said. "I won't see you hurt again. I thought about striking his name from the guest list, but, as the new countess of Howland, I must at least attempt connection with the only other title in the area."

"Very wise," Hester said. "And I'm glad you didn't. His sister, Elizabeth, is delightful. I know you'll like her. And he is…tolerable, as Rebecca says."

"Tolerable." Rosemary rolled the word around on her tongue. "Well, I guess I will have to be content at that. Just make sure you guard your heart this time, Hester."

Easier said than done, particularly at a wedding.

Hester had attended several weddings in the little chapel of St. Andrew's, including the one for her brother and Jesslyn. No other wedding had surpassed the number of attendees. Some of the villagers had waited outside the packed church to offer their best wishes to their spa hostess and daughter of their former physician.

The Earl of Howland had planned a smaller affair. His family—including his mother, the dowager countess; his daughter, Lady Miranda; Eva Howland, his cousin's wife; and the earl's aunt, Mrs. Marjorie Howland—filled the first pew near the stained-glass windows his ancestors had donated. His servants filled the last three rows on that side. Lark, Jesslyn, Aunt Maudie, and Jesslyn's brother, Alexander Chance, sat behind Hester's mother on the opposite side of the aisle along with friends from the villages, such as Abigail and her husband, the spa physician;

Mr. Carroll; and Mrs. Mance. The magistrate stood up with the earl as his attendant and witness.

And then there was Rob. From her place off the vestibule, Hester saw him and Elizabeth attempt to slip into the back row on Rosemary's side of the church, but her assistant teacher motioned him forward.

"You should be the guest of honor, my lord," Mrs. Mance whispered loud enough for Hester to hear. "You must sit higher."

Rob had looked around, met Hester's gaze, and winked before leading Elizabeth closer to Lark and Jesslyn.

Hester's cheeks heated. She busied herself in making sure the bow on Rebecca's silky dress was secure. Mrs. Peters, their nurse, had gathered Rebecca's curls into a cluster behind her head and tied them with a ribbon the same color as the gown. The little girl looked almost grown up. Hester's eyes misted.

Beside her, Rosemary fanned herself with one gloved hand, her own cheeks pink.

"You look breathtaking," Hester assured her, straightening to eye the silver-grey gown with its simple lines and dusting of lace across the bodice and along the hem.

"I feel breath*less*," Rosemary said. "Oh, for some vinaigrette just now."

Rebecca held up her reed basket of red autumn leaves. "You could sniff these."

With a smile, Rosemary bent over the basket, then straightened. "Thank you, sweetheart. That was just right."

As she paused, the quiet bore down on them. Hester turned with a jerk to find the entire congregation watching them, waiting. The vicar wiggled his fingers, beckoning her and Rosemary. It was time.

"Off you go, now," she whispered to Rebecca. "Just like we talked about."

Rebecca started down the center aisle, head high, basket steady, and steps stately.

"Ready?" Hester asked Rosemary.

Her sister beamed at her. "More than ready. You lead, and I'll follow."

Hester raised her head and stepped into the aisle. For much of her life, she had led, and her little sister had followed. But Rosemary's studies with their uncle had separated them, and Rob's romance and Hester's marriage had only widened the gap. Now Rosemary would be even farther away, as she started a family of her own.

Yet Hester could not begrudge her sister finding love. Rosemary deserved to be happy. That the earl intended to do everything in his power to make her happy was evident by the tender look on his handsome face as he watched her approach.

Rebecca reached the altar and turned to the right as planned, but she walked past the door of the pew her grandmother was holding open for her. Hester hurried her steps just the slightest to try to intercept her daughter, but it was too late.

Rebecca pushed on the door to the third pew down and slipped in to sit beside Rob.

Elizabeth stared at the little girl, then narrowed her eyes at Rob. "Was this planned?" she hissed.

Rob shook his head even as Hester's daughter snuggled up against him, still clutching her basket of scarlet autumn leaves. He glanced up to meet Hester's wide, panicked gaze. The last thing she and her sister needed right now was to worry about anything.

He sent her a nod and a smile to let her know he had this well in hand.

If only he believed that.

Rebecca gave a happy sigh. "I like weddings. Do you?"

"Yes," he whispered. "Now, watch to see what happens next."

Elizabeth shook her head as well before bowing it to join the vicar in the opening prayer of the service.

In truth, he hadn't attended all that many weddings. His older brother hadn't yet chosen a bride, and many of Rob's friends were avoiding getting leg-shackled until they'd had their fill of frivolity. Still, he hadn't realized the celebration would be such a solemn occasion, with a great deal of pontificating by the vicar between recited vows by the happy couple.

Who truly did look besotted.

The vicar was partway through his sermon when Rebecca began fidgeting. She set her basket on the pew, rearranged the leaves to her liking, set it on the floor, then picked it up again. Some of the attendees from across the aisle frowned in his direction, as if certain he had something to do with her behavior. Perhaps he did. But how did one go about occupying a six-year-old child?

He nudged her with his elbow, and she directed her big blue eyes to his face. Rob put a finger to his lips, then dropped his hand below the top of the pew to form something approximating a rabbit's head with his fingers and thumb. Rebecca's eyes widened.

He hopped the head closer to her, then away, and she watched avidly. When he hopped it closer again, she snatched at it. Rob jerked out of reach. She stilled, waiting.

The second time, she grabbed him and held on tight. "Got you!"

"Sh!" some lady from behind them warned.

Rebecca glanced over her shoulder. Rob pulled out of her grip and bounced the bunny away.

She caught him three more times before the vicar invited the congregation to acknowledge the Earl and

Countess of Howland.

As Rob rose, he met the gaze of Mrs. Greer, who was frowning at him as if wondering how the paragon she'd praised could have allowed a little girl to disrupt the service.

"I should like to see you remain silent, madam," he said, "if you caught a rabbit in church."

She blinked so rapidly he was certain the candles flickered with the breeze.

The earl and his bride made their way down the aisle to congratulations on all sides. Hester followed on the magistrate's arm. As she passed the pew, she held out her other hand for her daughter. Rebecca clung to Rob and shook her head.

For a moment, Hester looked stricken, as if he'd taken her last hope. Then she was past, and it was all he could do not to shout after her.

"Why didn't you want to go with your mother, Rebecca?" he asked.

She glanced up at him. "They're all so big."

He remembered that feeling. His brother and Elizabeth had reached their heights early. For a few years, Rob had been the shortest member of the family. He had always felt as if they were all looking down on him.

"We can fix that," he told her, and he bent and hefted her high in his arms, so her head was above even his.

"I can see Grandmother!" she cried.

As the church began to empty, Mrs. Denby came to join them. "Whatever were you thinking, Rebecca, to bother the viscount and Miss Peverell?"

Rebecca shrank against him. "I wasn't a bother."

"Indeed she was not," Rob assured her grandmother. "It was the most delightful service I have ever attended."

Elizabeth coughed into her hand. It sounded suspiciously like a laugh.

"That is very kind of you, my lord," Hester's mother

replied. "What do you say, Rebecca?"

Rebecca toyed with the velvet on his coat collar. "Will you come to the party? There will be dancing."

"Well, then, I wouldn't want to miss it," Rob told her.

Her grandmother held out her arms. "Come now, Rebecca."

Rebecca met his gaze. "Do I have to?"

Her grandmother drew herself up, for a proper scold, no doubt.

"You should," Rob said. "Your grandmother would probably very much like to spend this special day with her beloved granddaughter."

Her head swiveled. "Am I your beloved granddaughter, Grandmother?"

Mrs. Denby's round face melted. "Oh, sweetheart, of course. Now, hurry! What would the wedding party be without the attendant who carried the basket?"

Rob set her down, and she slipped her hand into her grandmother's. He thought she would abandon him without another thought, but she glanced back. "Come along, Lord Peverell."

"It seems you've been summoned by the queen," Elizabeth murmured beside him as Rebecca skipped out, hand in her grandmother's, seemingly without a doubt that he would follow.

"Would you mind attending for a while?" Rob asked.

Her smile was content. "I'll be fine. I didn't notice Mr. Donner in the crowd, but surely someone will be willing to dance with me."

She'd been looking for Donner? Guilt sank its teeth into him. He'd explained to his sister that the fellow had requested a moment of his time to ask about a business arrangement rather than suggest a courtship, but apparently that hadn't stopped Elizabeth from hoping. He'd have to have another word with the agent the next time they met. And he still needed to have a conversation about the possible capture of the Lord of the Smugglers.

For now, they exited the church and rode up to the assembly rooms for the wedding breakfast. He'd never understood why the celebration was called a breakfast when it might be held even in the middle of the afternoon as it was today, but that didn't stop him from enjoying the roast tongue, baked ham, sweet rolls, and other delicacies the footmen served to the guests at tables set across the top of the hall. For all Howland was hurting financially, he hadn't skimped on feeding his guests.

Rob's rank allowed him a prime place near the head table, where the bride, groom, and their families congregated. It also allowed him a prime view of Hester. She'd styled her hair so that little tendrils curled around her cheeks, caressing them in a way he'd once had leave to do. The warm color of her dress matched the color of her lips. She kept her head down, seeing to Rebecca's needs, conversing with the little girl. No matter how long he watched, he couldn't seem to will her to raise her head and favor him with a glance.

"You should ask her to dance," Elizabeth said as a quartet began warming up in the musicians' alcove above the main floor.

Rob dragged his gaze back to his sister. "The bride and new countess? I'm certain her husband might have something to say about that."

"You can pretend to misunderstand me all you like," his sister warned. "But if you don't ask Hester, someone else will, and I refuse to see you moping about again."

Rob tore open a sweet roll with his fingers. "I do not mope."

"Or frown prodigiously, apparently." She nodded to where Rebecca had wiggled off her mother's lap to go speak to the earl's daughter. "You could always ask Rebecca instead. She seems to like you. I can't imagine why."

Neither could he.

In the end, he girded up his loins to approach Hester. She was laughing over something her sister had said, and he wanted to sit and soak up the sound. Unfortunately, it shut off abruptly as she glanced his way at last.

He bowed. "Mrs. Todd. Would you care to dance?"

She regarded him a moment, and he held his breath.

"I fear I've eaten too much of the earl's fine ham," she said, and he sagged with disappointment.

"But I'm certain you're not too full for a promenade, dear," her mother put in.

Bless the woman.

Hester pasted on a smile. "Indeed. I would enjoy a promenade, if you'd care to join me, my lord."

"To the ends of the earth and beyond," he vowed, offering her his arm.

Her brow went up as she rose, but she lay her hand on his, and they set off. He rather thought he was strutting. How little encouragement it took from her to change his whole outlook.

"What have you done to my daughter?" she asked as they strolled along the edge of the dancefloor, where other couples were beginning to gather. "I don't recall her ever sitting so quietly through a service."

At least Mrs. Greer, who was now seated farther down the tables, hadn't told tales as yet. "Rebecca is a delight and a credit to you."

She regarded him. "That still doesn't explain her affinity for you."

He shrugged. "What can I say? Women find me attractive."

She choked. "Girls may find you attractive, my lord. Ladies are something else entirely."

"I will not quibble," he said as they circled the bottom of the room. It simply felt too good to have her on his arm, as if she were meant to be there. "Weddings, apparently, put one in a good mood."

"They do." She glanced to where the earl and her sister were now stepping out to lead the first set.

"I don't suppose you know anyone else who's marrying soon?" he ventured.

Mouth hinting of a smile, she shook her head. "Alas, no."

He heaved a sigh. "A shame. I thought that might be one way you'd consent to dance with your old friend again."

The smile won. "Yes, and you are such an *old* friend."

Rob grimaced. "I'll have you know I am not in my dotage, madam."

"Noted," she said. "Though I begin to wonder whether you are set in your ways, above such things as romance and adventure now."

He leaned closer, until he could inhale the apple spice of her fragrance. "I could prove you wrong with one kiss."

Color flamed in her cheeks. Oh, to reach out his hand, touch the soft warmth. Instead, he made himself look away, keeping his steps steady and composed.

"Really, sir," she said. "Perhaps you are still too bold after all."

Rob inclined his head. "Then I must beg your pardon and say no more on the matter."

"Promise?"

He glanced at her to find a twinkle in her blue-green eyes. He drew himself up in mock offense. "Do you imply that I speak too much?"

"On occasion?" she suggested.

"Well, then, I will close my mouth and not speak another word in your presence."

She eyed him.

"I mean it. Not another word. Ever."

She waited.

"Test me. Try me. I will prevail."

She cocked her head.

"Do you doubt me, madam? Name your second."

She gave it up and laughed. Oh, for a taste of that joy. He wanted to roll it around inside him, enjoying every moment.

"What am I to do with you?" she asked.

Several suggestions sprang to mind, all no doubt stemming from his previous life, for none were particularly appropriate for her sister's wedding.

"I am a sad trial," he acknowledged.

She sighed. "I suspect you are right."

Rob gave her a contrite smile. "But I'm trying so hard to improve. Can you not grant me the least concession?"

She was quiet a moment, and he thought he might have pushed her too hard. Then she nodded. "I can do nothing today, sir, but if you were to ride out the coast path on Saturday around half past eleven, you might find company waiting."

She was offering him an assignation? His pulse quickened. "I'll be there. I promise."

CHAPTER ELEVEN

THE WEDDING BREAKFAST DIDN'T END until the sun was setting. Hester couldn't help noticing that Rob and his sister had been among the last to leave. He'd finished the promenade with her and bowed himself off, grinning so broadly it was a wonder her mother hadn't commented on the matter.

Hester shook her head as she led Rebecca for the coach. What had she been thinking to invite him to ride? She'd have to make an excuse to her mother and Rebecca, borrow a horse from the livery stable. What if her riding habit no longer fit?

What if a moment alone in Rob's company made her reckless?

No, no. She was stronger now, even if spending time in his company made her feel alive, appreciated, and admired again.

Still, she hadn't been able to convince herself to dance with him at the wedding breakfast.

In truth, she had been afraid what her face might reveal. It was all too easy to think of romance when all around her couples were billing and cooing. She couldn't remember acting so besotted with Jasper at their small wedding at St. Mary's in Upper Grace, but then, she hadn't been besotted. Just happy to have someone care about her most of all.

Was Rob capable of putting anyone before himself? He'd agreed to her suggestion of a promenade rather than a dance and they called themselves friends. He had been very good to sit with Rebecca during the wedding. But he could be spending time with her and her family because he found them companionable. Unlike Mrs. Greer and some of the others in Grace-by-the-Sea, they asked nothing of him.

"What a lovely day," her mother said with a sigh as they settled into the carriage for the return to Upper Grace. The earl and Rosemary were on their way to Lyme Regis for a short honeymoon, and Mr. and Mrs. Inchley and their family were already setting the assembly rooms to rights.

"It was," Hester agreed. Beside her, Rebecca yawned, then lay her head in Hester's lap. Hester pulled the ribbon free and stroked the soft blond curls.

"Everyone was so kind," her mother continued. "The countess, the earl, the magistrate and his wife. Lord Peverell."

Hester glanced down at her daughter. Rebecca's eyes had drifted shut and her breath came softly. "Yes," Hester acknowledged. "Everyone was very kind."

"I was glad to see you encourage him," her mother said. "How nice if you should have a home of your own."

She'd thought she had a home of her own, but of course, the house she and Rebecca lived in now belonged to her mother. Still, she hadn't thought herself there on sufferance.

"Are Rebecca and I a burden, Mother?" she asked.

Immediately her mother shook her head, dislodging some of her own curls. "No, of course not! But I was happiest in my marriage. Look how happy Rosemary is. I thought you were happy with Lieutenant Todd. If Lord Peverell should offer an opportunity, you should take it."

"Do you think he'd make a good husband?" Hester

challenged.

Her mother waved a hand. "I haven't seen anything the least objectionable since he's returned. He seems quite settled into his role as viscount."

"But how can you be sure?" Hester pressed. "What if it's just a game to him? What if he's playing a part until he can return to London?"

Her mother frowned as the coach rumbled across the Downs under a sky that was growing heavier with rain. "And what if he isn't? If his generous donations don't sway you, look at how he cares for his sister. Look at how he treats Rebecca, for that matter. I don't understand why you won't try to know him better."

She could give her a dozen reasons, but only if she wanted her past shame known. "I must think of Rebecca."

Her mother glanced at her granddaughter asleep on Hester's lap. "I think it's quite clear that Rebecca likes him very much indeed."

Her daughter certainly did. Hester wasn't sure why. She managed to turn the conversation in the coach to other things until they reached home and she was able to carry Rebecca up to the nursery.

Nurse Peters had cared for the children of half the gentry in Upper Grace. Of an age with Hester's mother, she tutted over Rebecca as Hester came into the suite they now used as the nursery, her brown eyes soft and head cocked so her white cap tilted on her brown hair.

"There's a sweet little girl. Did she have a good time at the wedding?"

"An excellent time," Hester assured her, laying her daughter on the bed. "Let me help you settle her."

Together, they worked at removing Rebecca's polished leather slippers and white wool stockings. Her daughter opened her eyes as Hester lifted her so Nurse Peters could work on her clothing.

"We're home?" Rebecca asked, glancing around.

"Indeed we are," Hester said. "Help Nurse with your pretty dress."

Rebecca obediently lifted her arms so the nurse could pull the confection off her.

"May I wear it to church on Sunday?" she asked Hester as Mrs. Peters went to lay it aside.

"Church sounds like a very good choice for that dress," Hester agreed, tugging the nightgown over her daughter's head.

"Will Lord Peverell be there?" Rebecca asked.

Hester focused on settling the soft folds around her daughter. "He attends St. Andrew's, remember? We attend St. Mary's."

Rebecca's face was turning an unbecoming red, her mouth set. "We could go to St. Andrew's."

Nurse Peters glanced Hester's way, then hurried to turn down the covers on the bed.

Hester lowered her voice. "You want to attend St. Andrew's because you like Lord Peverell."

"Yes." Such surety in that one word.

"Why do you like him?" Hester asked.

Rebecca yawned again before answering. "He's pretty."

Nurse Peters barked a laugh and hurriedly swallowed it. Hester had to bite her lips a moment to keep from laughing herself.

"Gentlemen are generally described as handsome, not pretty," she explained to her daughter as Rebecca climbed under the covers.

Rebecca frowned. "Why?"

"I'm not sure," Hester allowed, pulling the blankets up around her. "But I agree that Lord Peverell is handsome."

"He's nice too," Rebecca continued, settling on her pillow.

"Because he gives you things," Hester guessed.

"He plays with me," Rebecca disagreed. "And he's nice to his sister. I wish I had a sister."

All at once, Hester could picture her—a little girl with tousled hair and hazel eyes. Rob's eyes. It was all she could do to say prayers with Rebecca and retreat to her own room next door. Even then, sleep was a long time coming.

The very air tasted sweeter to Rob, knowing he would be seeing Hester on Saturday. He wasn't sure what had prompted her to make the offer, but he hadn't been about to refuse. If that made him less like the viscount he planned to be, he could live with that, for now.

In the meantime, he had an unexpected visitor.

Bascom came up to announce him Friday morning, at a time entirely too early for calls if they had been in London. Indeed, Elizabeth still wore her morning gown, a frothy muslin creation with a great profusion of lace and ribbon.

"There's a gentleman to see you, my lord," the footman said when Elizabeth acknowledged Bascom standing in the doorway of their mother's withdrawing room. "Captain St. Claire, formerly of His Majesty's Navy and currently residing in Dove Cottage."

Elizabeth set aside the book she had been reading. "Captain St. Claire? All of the ladies have remarked on him. Show him up, Bascom, by all means."

Rob frowned at her, but his young footman shifted from foot to foot. "Begging your pardon, miss, but he asked to be shown into his lordship's study. I don't think he wanted to talk to you."

Elizabeth's face turned pink, and she picked up her book again. "Very well. It isn't as if I wanted him to call anyway."

"I'll only be a moment," Rob promised, edging for the

door.

"Was I wrong, my lord?" Bascom whispered as they started down the stairs. "I only did what the captain ordered."

"And you are used to obeying the orders of a captain, I suppose," Rob said, eyeing him.

The fellow kept his gaze on his feet, as if the stair treads were not to be trusted. "Aye, my lord. I am. But I work for you now, and if I misstepped, I'm sorry."

Propitiating to keep his position? Or hiding his intentions? Rob still wasn't sure of him, but he followed Bascom to his study.

A tall, raven-haired fellow was standing by the windows, looking out over the rear yard. He turned as Rob entered the room and nodded, as if Rob were the one who had come to see him.

"Captain St. Claire," Rob said, moving forward and extending his hand. "To what do I owe this pleasure?"

Dark, hooded eyes regarded him as the captain shook hands with a firm grip. "I'd like to speak to you about your pier."

In the act of withdrawing his hand, Rob hesitated, then recovered. With his dark hair, flashing eyes, and military bearing, this could easily be Donner's Lord of the Smugglers. Yet Hester vowed the fellow had been caught.

But he could not deny St. Claire had a lordly air about him as he sauntered to the chair in front of Rob's desk and deigned to sit. Head up, he regarded Rob as if inviting him to do the same. With a shake of his head, Rob sat behind the desk.

"And what interest do you have in my pier?" he asked his guest. "I understand you were formerly in His Majesty's Navy. Are you awaiting reassignment?"

"Recovering from a wound," he explained, making a show of rubbing his left knee. "And I do a little sailing to reaccustom myself to life aboard ship. It's not always convenient to bring my vessel, the *Siren's Call*, into Grace Cove. I will admit that on occasion I have docked her below the Lodge, when you and your charming sister were not in residence. I was hoping you might be willing to extend me that courtesy in the coming days."

So, he admitted to using the pier. Had that blue flash last week been from his ship? Had he placed Bascom on Rob's staff to respond? Then why pretend civility and ask?

"I suppose that could be arranged," Rob said. "We have no ship at the moment. When would you have need of the pier? The dark of the moon, perhaps?"

St. Claire smiled. "Perhaps. And I'll be sure to leave something for my gallant host."

"I prefer champagne," Rob tried.

"That's hard to come by," St. Claire mused. "Us being at war with France and all. But I'll see what I can do." He rose and inclined his head. "Thank you for your time, my lord. I'll see myself out."

Rob nodded, and the fellow strolled from the room.

Leaning back in the chair, Rob gazed out at the rear yard, but instead of sunlight on the Channel, he saw men creeping across the grass by moonlight, arms filled with illicit goods.

He needed to talk to Donner, tell him about St. Claire's request. And he needed to talk to Mr. Chalder, his night watchman, because he had a feeling there would be far more activity in the next few days than anyone had expected.

Even Rob, as it turned out.

Mercer arrived late that afternoon with more papers regarding the estate. Rob spent a long two hours reviewing and approving the movement of investments, the improvement of properties, and the leases of various holdings.

"And I believe we had a request for the use of the pier

on occasion, my lord," Mercer said as he filed the signed papers in his portfolio where he stood beside Rob like a schoolmaster.

How had the fellow learned so quickly? "From Captain St. Claire," Rob agreed, straightening his shoulders with an audible crack after hunching over the desk. "He approached me this morning. I approved."

Mercer blinked. "The request did not come from Captain St. Claire, my lord. Another local fellow made the request, a fisherman, I believe."

Rob frowned up at him. His steward was ever the fastidious one, from the crisp cut of his coat to the way he doled out his benighted papers.

"You believe?" Rob challenged. "I would expect you to have looked into the matter more fully, Mercer, so that you would *know*."

He clutched his portfolio closer, look chiding Rob for his lack of faith. "I did, my lord. Captain Ruggins sailed out of Weymouth and brought in loads of mackerel on a regular basis. He retired a few months ago but is finding himself ill at ease without a purpose each day."

"Wouldn't Grace Cove be more suitable as an anchorage for a fishing vessel, then?" Rob questioned. "We hardly want wagons rumbling over the rear yard with mackerel."

Mercer grimaced. "I believe, that is, he relayed that he will be taking his cargo along the shore to the west. Your pier is more conducive to such an arrangement than the cove."

"Very well," Rob said. "He may use the pier during the day. Captain St. Claire may use it at night."

"At night?" Mercer asked, shifting on his feet. "Why would the captain be sailing at night?"

Rob regarded him, counting off the seconds until his steward's brows rose.

"Oh, Lord Peverell," he protested, "I thought we agreed

you would not ally yourself with smugglers. Captain Ruggins is a far better option, and I am sure he'd appreciate night landings as well. One never knows when the fish will be biting, after all."

Rob rather thought a good fisherman knew exactly where and when the fish would be biting. This Captain Ruggins began to sound even more suspicious than St. Claire.

"Perhaps I should meet this captain," he ventured. "See what I think of the fellow."

Mercer readjusted his portfolio, as if it were poking him under the arm. "He would not presume to meet you, my lord. He is fully aware of his humble background, which is why he enlisted my aid to make his petition. I would be happy to send word to Captain St. Claire and explain that the use of the pier has already been taken."

"Or," Rob told him, "you could send word to Captain Ruggins that I have decided to favor St. Claire with the concession. And I begin to wonder if I should charge for the honor."

Mercer puffed out a sigh as if much put out by the decision. "Captain Ruggins may be amenable to leaving you some of his catch to pay for the use of the pier."

Rob shrugged. "Captain St. Claire promised me champagne."

Mercer glanced each way as if he thought anyone might be listening, then lowered his head and his voice. "I could request that Captain Ruggins do the same."

Rob crossed his arms over his chest. "Out with it, Mercer. For all your posturing, you know that Captain Ruggins is a smuggler too."

"I would not claim so, my lord," Mercer rushed to assure him. The sweat dotting his brow called him liar. "But there is a slight possibility. Many a sailor along this coast has been tempted."

Rob eyed him. "What did he promise if you secured

the concession?"

Mercer snatched the last page off the desk. "Nothing of any import. A gentleman's agreement only. And it matters not, as it appears I was too late. Now, I must be going, so I can return to London and file these papers."

Rob nodded, and his man of affairs scurried from the room as if the Lord of the Smugglers were on his tail.

Which, perhaps, he was.

Rob rose to go find his sister. Bascom, on duty by the front door, pointed him to the withdrawing room Rob's mother had favored.

"She is entertaining, my lord," he explained. "Mr. Donner called."

"Did he?" The words must have come out more growl than he intended, for the footman blanched.

Rob took the stairs two at a time and plowed into the withdrawing room just as Donner reached for his sister's hand. The fellow yanked back his fingers as if he'd been burned.

"Rob," Elizabeth greeted him. "You remember Mr. Donner."

"Donner, Donner," Rob mused, moving to stand in front of them. "It's been so long. Have we met recently?"

Donner had the good sense to color. "Forgive me, my lord. I was detained."

Elizabeth glanced between them. "I don't understand. Were you expecting Mr. Donner to call, Rob?"

"Frequently," Rob said. "On your feet, sir. I have words for you."

"Rob, no!" Elizabeth surged up in a rustle of lavender muslin as her would-be beau stood as well. "He's done nothing wrong."

"We'll see about that," Rob said. "My study, sir. Now."

He turned and stalked from the room.

Donner must have followed, for he was on Rob's heels as Rob pushed open the door to the study and motioned him inside.

"Nicely done," Donner said as he closed the door behind him. "You sound exactly like an over-protective brother."

"Because I am an over-protective brother," Rob informed him. "I told you to leave my sister out of this, yet you persist in furthering the tale of your interest in her."

Donner shook his head. "Your sister cares nothing for me. I know how these flirtations go. I'm merely someone to enliven her time in rustication."

The truth bit hard. He'd used Hester in just such a way. But his sister was someone else entirely.

"You're wrong," Rob told him. "If my sister shows interest in you, it is because she *is* interested in you. We neither of us have ever considered station more important than character and commitment."

He paled. "I see. Then I apologize, my lord. I would never want to see your sister hurt."

"On that we agree. So I will ask your intentions."

He reared back. "My intentions? You'd allow me to have intentions?"

Rob rolled his eyes. "My opinion on the matter has no bearing whatsoever. It is what Elizabeth wants that counts. If my sister would welcome a courtship, would you be willing to entertain one?"

"No, certainly not. But she wouldn't, she couldn't. I'm not worthy of her."

"It seems we agree on that as well."

When Donner dropped his gaze and shuffled his feet, Rob sighed. "Oh, sit down, man. I need your attention on a matter of more interest to the War Office."

His head snapped up. "The Lord of the Smugglers has approached you."

"Two possible Lord of the Smugglers have approached me," Rob informed him, going for his desk. "Even though

I have been assured the fellow was captured months ago."

"You speak of Henry Bascom," Donner said, taking the seat opposite him. "Some here considered him the Lord of the Smugglers, but we in the War Office quickly determined he wasn't our man."

"How?" Rob demanded, leaning both hands on the desk.

Donner's smile was smug. "Information continued to flow, all attributed to this puffed up brigand."

"Could someone else have assumed his mantle?" Rob asked.

"Possibly. Regardless, the fellow is not to be trusted."

"Then we need to determine which one is our man," Rob said.

Donner nodded. "I'll alert the War Office, see if any new information has come to light. In the meantime, keep your eyes open, my lord. Together, we will catch the villain in the act."

CHAPTER TWELVE

HESTER WASN'T CERTAIN HOW SHE'D func-tion until Saturday, so great was her anticipation at meeting Rob. At least teaching on Friday kept her mind occupied. She and Mrs. Mance organized a spelling competition that had the children shouting out answers for a chance to be named the winner. A few people in the village had complained to the rector that the children didn't need to know how to write, but she and Rosemary had agreed that reading, and writing, were important, whatever occupation a person might someday practice.

Saturday at half-past eleven, she was waiting on the coast path, perched on her sidesaddle atop a bay mare she had borrowed from the Upper Grace livery stable, sharp, briny breeze tugging at her navy riding skirts. She hadn't wanted to lie to her mother again, so she'd confided she was going riding with Rob. Her mother had been elated.

"Borrow your sister's hat," she'd advised. "The tall-crowned one wrapped in tulle with the crimson band."

"That hat is probably sitting somewhere in Castle How," Hester had reminded her, "if Rosemary didn't take it on her honeymoon. I'm just thankful my riding habit still fits. It's been a long time since I rode for sport."

Her mother had been teary-eyed once more as Hester had left. Why had she allowed the dear lady to get her hopes up? It was just a ride.

Yet it felt like so much more.

She shook her head. It might be just the two of them, but it was hardly intimate. They were out of doors, along a path frequented by farmers. And this heavy-boned mare with her long legs could probably outrun anything he had brought with him from London, so she could escape whenever she liked.

Still, all at once, it was seven years ago, and she was waiting for him to come to her across the Downs.

When he appeared, her heart soared.

He too had forsaken a hat, so that the breeze brushed his tawny hair back from his face. His crimson riding coat was tailored to give those broad shoulders room to move, and the chamois breeches hugged his legs. Her pulse was pounding faster than his horse's hooves as he drew near and reined in.

"Good day, Hester," he called, smile warmer than the simple words warranted. "Fine day for a ride."

"At the moment," she allowed. She tipped her chin down the Channel, toward where the Isle of Portland could be seen jutting out into the blue-grey waters. "But see those clouds to the west? We'll have rain by tonight."

"Then we should enjoy ourselves while we can," he said. "Which way would you care to go?"

West took them entirely too close to home. "East," she said, and they set off at a walk across the browning grasses. A tree here and there reveled in its autumn color, saffron and russet. Sheep with black faces glanced up to watch them pass.

"Quiet out here," he ventured as they crossed the field.

"Now," she acknowledged. "But you should have seen the area a few weeks ago when the farmers were trying to get in the hay before the rains came. Some of my older students had to stay home and either help or watch younger ones so both parents could work."

"And now these fields are my responsibility," he mused,

gaze going off across the Downs. "I didn't think about it when Father was alive: all our properties, all our tenants. Mercer, our steward, tells me we have more than two hundred people depending on us, and that doesn't count their children. As viscount, I must see to their wellbeing."

Hester raised her brows. "No one man can care for more than two hundred people."

By the way his shoulders slumped, he had been trying to do just that. "I have a team of men at each location and Mercer to oversee them. But he still brings all decisions to me. I find it a remarkably heavy burden."

She didn't need Rosemary's lorgnette to see that. Even his eyes sagged with the weight of it. "What will you do?"

His smile was sad. "What can I do? I am the viscount. I must rise to the occasion. There is no one else."

She reached across the distance and brushed his shoulder with her hand. "You have always been clever. You'll find a way. It might not be the way of your father or brother, but it will suffice."

He nodded, then straightened, and her hand fell back.

"Enough of the maudlin," he declared. "See that tree up ahead?"

Hester followed his gaze to the wide-spreading branches of an oak, the leaves crimson now with autumn. "Yes. What about it?"

"How fast can we reach it?"

"How fast?" Hester asked, fingers tightening on the reins. "Do you mean to race?"

The charming smile she remembered popped into view. "Of course. The first one to pass the tree wins a kiss."

Heat thrummed through her veins. She should refuse. She must refuse.

She didn't want to refuse.

"From whomever she chooses," she amended. "You're

on." She clapped her heel against the bay's side, and the mare leaped forward. Over the thundering hooves, she thought she heard Rob's cry.

She bent forward, urged the mare faster. The wind stung her cheeks, pulled her hair from her pins to send it streaming away from her face. The thunder grew louder as Rob's horse pounded closer.

"Come on, girl," she urged. "Just a little farther."

She passed the tree in a flash, then slowed her mount to circle back.

Rob was waiting for her, smile proud.

"You won," he said. "I am ready to surrender my kiss."

That look declared as much. His gaze roamed over her face to fix upon her lips.

"I said the lady may choose whom she kisses," she reminded him, giving her mount a pat and willing her heart to cease its frantic beat. "What if I were to choose Rebecca?"

He crumpled over his saddle. "Rebecca! Ah, to have come so close to perfection and fallen short."

Hester laughed. "You were the one to suggest a race."

He straightened and edged his mount closer. "But you decided the true winner. Can I say nothing to convince you to change your mind? Kissing me might be more invigorating than kissing your daughter."

She remembered. She was leaning toward him before she thought better of it.

He met her halfway. His lips brushed hers, soft and gentle. His sigh tingled against her mouth. Oh, the delight, the joy, the wonder.

Her mare was wiser than she was, for the horse moved away from Rob's, breaking the kiss. Hester gathered her dignity with the reins. "It seems we are not above old habits."

"You are far more than an old habit," he murmured, gaze caressing her face. "You are the very air I breathe."

So easy to fall into that gaze, into those arms.

"Those are not the words of a friend, sir," she said primly.

"Perhaps not," he allowed. "Perhaps I want more."

Her pulse would not be still. But if he could issue a challenge, so could she.

"What more can there be between a viscount and a widow teaching at a dame school?" she demanded.

"That," he said, "is entirely up to you."

Was it? So little in her life had seemed her choice. She had not chosen to move to Upper Grace on her father's death. She had not chosen for Rob to leave her behind. She had agreed to marry Jasper, but she certainly hadn't chosen to be left a widow. Even her teaching job was only because Rosemary had been deemed unsuitable.

"I think it is something the two of us must decide," she countered. "For a lady like myself, when it comes to a gentleman, there is friendship, and there is courtship. If you will not have the one, are you willing to consider the other? Only you can answer that, Rob."

He was silent, gazing at her with that yearning in his eyes, and all of her cried out. She hadn't been good enough for him then. It seemed she wasn't good enough for him now. Why had she thought things might be different between them?

Once more, she clapped her heel to her mount and fled, but this time *she* left *him* behind.

He wasn't as clever as she'd named him, for all Rob could do was sit in the saddle and stare as Hester's horse carried her away from him. Her question had caught him off guard. He'd been too stunned to think.

He could pursue her, but he hadn't been able to catch

her the first time they'd raced a few minutes ago. He doubted he could catch her the second. And, if he did manage to catch her, what would he say to her?

Was he willing to court her, to marry her, to be a husband and father?

He certainly wasn't making a very good viscount. He'd eagerly agreed to this meeting when he was to weigh all decisions. He must protect his holdings, his tenants and staff, and his family.

He also had to secure his line.

There was that. The Peverell lineage had gone from having an heir and a spare, as some called it, to Rob being the last. No distant cousin waited in the wings, to his knowledge. Perhaps the College of Heralds might be able to scare one up, but where did that leave Elizabeth?

So, wasn't it his duty to marry?

The rain she'd predicted pattered across the ground, pebbling him with ice. Humbled and thoughtful, he turned his mount for home.

Elizabeth spotted him from the withdrawing room as he was heading for his bedchamber.

"I won't ask you how your ride went," she said, raising a brow. "It's written all over your face."

"Then perhaps I should wash my face," he grumbled, turning to go change out of his sodden riding clothes.

"Perhaps you should," she called after him. "And when you're done, join me in the library. We must talk."

Rob paused and glanced back. "Everything all right?"

"Most assuredly not when my brother's countenance is stormier than the autumn skies. I'll be waiting for the full story." She wiggled her brows as if she expected high entertainment.

She was doomed to disappointment.

He allowed Eckman, his valet, to take his time changing him into fresh breeches and coat. Delaying tactics. What was he to say to his sister? From the moment Hester had bumped into him at the Harvest Ball, Elizabeth had been pushing him toward her. She'd claimed to have seen something between him and Hester. She'd be saddened to find it might be too little, too late.

His sister was standing with a book in her hand as he entered the room. An ancestor had included a library in their summer retreat, and another had stocked it with a few weighty tomes like the nineteen-volume *Rise and Fall of the Roman Empire* and Colquhoun's various treatises on social ills in London, as if trying to impress upon any visitors the serious nature of the house's inhabitants.

It didn't help that the room was paneled in dark wood, with a single narrow window high in one wall and a black carpet with bronze-colored chess pieces emblazoned on it covering most of the polished wood floor. His father and mother, bless them, had added novels, poetry, and plays and brought in plenty of brass lamps. He'd often found Elizabeth curled up in one of the leather-bound armchairs, lost in a story, when she was younger.

And promptly chivied her out the door into the sunshine.

"Wordsworth?" he asked as he came into the room now.

"Blake," she said, lowering the book. "You look better. Was that sufficient time to reconsider your misbehavior?"

"How do you know I misbehaved?" he argued, going to sit on one of the other chairs.

Elizabeth collapsed onto the one nearest her, grey skirts puddling on the thick carpet. "Because you always misbehave. And I doubt Hester has it in her."

"You'd be wrong there," he said, leaning back and studying the scene on the curved ceiling. Plump peasants merrily stomped grapes under a heavy sky while tables groaned with crusty loaves and clay jars brimming with olives. Now, wouldn't that be a fine place to learn to be the head of the family?

"Really?" Elizabeth pressed. "She seems quite proper."

Rob dropped his gaze to his sister to find her eyeing him again. "She is a lady through and through. But she didn't seem so wedded to the rules once."

The word wedded only served to remind him of their discussion. He found himself on his feet and moving about the room, which seemed somehow smaller and tighter than he remembered, as if the dark wood was closing in on him.

"And what rules is she determined that you follow now?" Elizabeth asked, turning her head as he passed her.

Rob clasped his hands behind his back. "I may have expressed my admiration for her too fervently, for she challenged me to prove it."

"Slaying a dragon?" Elizabeth suggested. "Finding the fabled lost treasures of the East?"

"Nothing so fantastical." Rob stopped and faced his sister fully. "She asked for courtship and commitment."

Elizabeth leaned back. "Well. I like her even more now."

Rob chuckled as he came back to his seat. "So do I. But can she be happy here?"

Elizabeth shrugged. "You know very well I have not always been happy here. And it isn't the Lodge that concerns you. It's London, the Season. Society."

He nodded. "All expectations for a viscountess."

"All expectations of a viscount," she told him. "You recall the years that Mother refused to go up for the Season, particularly when you and I were younger."

"I remember."

She narrowed her eyes, as if she thought he meant to refute her nonetheless. "Not every family participates as heavily as Father and Thomas. Some lords do not take their seats in Parliament."

"Such a fine excuse," Rob teased. "A shame I cannot feel comfortable taking it."

"Because you have changed," Elizabeth insisted.

He'd like to think he'd always had enough honor to do his duty. He'd simply never had such a duty before.

"So, you think it possible Hester and I might…" He could not make himself finish the sentence.

She beckoned with her hand as if to draw out the words. When he merely smiled, she shook her head. "You cannot even speak of it, Rob. You have no business courting a lady until you can."

"That's ridiculous." He rose to his full height and gazed down his nose at her. "I am prepared to court and marry, should I make the decision to do so."

Her mouth quirked. "And have you made such a decision?"

He grimaced. "Perhaps not yet."

"Ah." She stood and came to join him. "Then you simply need to become better acquainted with Hester. See if you suit."

"I feel as if I know her rather well already," Rob pointed out.

"You knew her well seven years ago," Elizabeth replied. "You must stop seeing the girl you loved and start seeing the woman right in front of you. Invite her and her mother to dinner. That will give you a better idea of how she fits in our world."

It was a simple step. It didn't commit him to anything. Yet it felt like a declaration.

One Hester deserved.

"Very well," Rob said. "Would you make the arrangements for me, send out the invitations?"

She smiled. "Delighted, Brother. But of course, we will be uneven numbers at table if I simply invite Hester and her mother. I'll have to invite a couple of gentlemen as well."

She'd sprung the trap so neatly he hadn't even seen it. "Gentlemen," he drawled.

"Yes, of course," Elizabeth said, all wide-eyed innocence. "We must have a partner for Mrs. Denby. What would you think of Lord Featherstone?"

"A fine fellow. And I suppose we must have a gentleman to accompany you as well."

"What a splendid idea," she said as if she hadn't planned it that way all along. "Mr. Donner might suffice. I must have someone to converse with while you make eyes at Hester."

Rob crossed his arms over his chest. "Why Donner? Surely there are other interesting fellows at the spa."

She made a face. "Fewer than you might think this time of year. And I like Mr. Donner. He makes me smile."

For that alone, he could bless the fellow. "Very well. But I must ask, Elizabeth: what are your feelings toward Donner?"

His forthright, self-assured sister dropped her gaze and set about straightening some of the books on the shelf. "He seems personable."

"That is not what I asked."

She was turned half away from him, but he could see the pink creeping into her cheek. "I told you I like him."

"Now who's avoiding commitment?"

She seized a book and turned to face him as if prepared to hurl it at him. "I am not opposed to commitment, but I will not be pushed into marriage by you or anyone else."

Rob held up his hands. "Far be it from me to disagree. You have an inheritance from Mother. You have reached your majority. You don't need my support or permission."

She set the book back into place more gently than she'd pulled it out. "Thank you. Now, let's talk more about this dinner party."

CHAPTER THIRTEEN

ROB HADN'T PURSUED HER. HESTER had hoped he might. She'd actually looked back once as she'd ridden off, but the grasses of the Downs had stretched away in the distance, barren and empty. Her life had felt as empty.

That was silly. She had a fine life. She was a mother, sister, daughter, and teacher. She made a difference. She thanked God for that when she, her mother, and Rebecca attended services at St. Mary's on Sunday. She thanked Him again as she spent the afternoon with her darling daughter. And she thanked Him once more as she lay down on her bed and tried to force thoughts of Rob Peverell from her mind at last.

Yet, as she returned to school on Monday, she could not help but notice that she wasn't as patient with Jimmy when he spoke out of turn in class. She wasn't nearly as cheerful when Mrs. Mance informed her that the village elders had agreed to fund the school another year. Nor was she as attentive as she walked Rebecca home, mind going to what might have been instead of what was, so that she had to ask her daughter to repeat herself.

That was intolerable. She would not allow Rob to come between her and Rebecca.

"Your birthday will be here soon," she reminded her daughter as they climbed the short stairs to the door of her mother's house. "What should we do to celebrate?"

Rebecca brightened as they entered the house. "A cake. With plums. Big enough for everyone."

"Everyone?" Hester asked with a smile, removing her bonnet. "How many people will be celebrating with us?"

"Aunt Rosemary, the earl, Lady Miranda, Jimmy," she rattled off before pausing for a breath. "And Lord Peverell."

Oh, her daughter could not know what hearing that name did to her equilibrium. "Lord Peverell will likely be too busy," Hester explained as she removed Rebecca's bonnet as well. "He may not even be visiting by then. He must return to his home in London."

Rebecca frowned. "He doesn't live in London. He has a big house on the cliff above St. Andrew's. Lady Miranda told me."

"That is his summer house," Hester explained. "His ancestral home is in Wiltshire, but he spends much of his time in London."

Her daughter's frown only grew. "He has *three* houses?"

He might have more, as far as Hester knew. He'd said he had over two hundred staff and tenants, after all.

"Think of them as places he sometimes is," she tried. "You're sometimes here, sometimes at church, and sometimes at school."

"Oh." She slipped her hand into Hester's as they started up the stairs. "Well, I hope he is sometimes here when it's my birthday."

"Hester!"

Her mother's urgent cry stopped her on the stairs. "Go up to Nurse Peters, Rebecca," she urged her daughter.

"Is Grandmother all right?" she asked, face puckering.

"Hester!" The name sounded positively breathless. "You must see this!"

"I'm sure she'll be fine," Hester promised, giving the girl a little push up the stairs. Rebecca hurried to the chamber story, and Hester plunged for the ground floor.

She found her mother in the sitting room, fanning herself with a missive. As soon as she saw Hester, she hurried forward in a flurry of spruce green wool and thrust the parchment at her.

"Well, go on," she demanded when Hester hesitated. "Read it. Oh, it is beyond anything."

Afraid of what she might find, Hester took the letter and scanned it. She'd thought perhaps there'd been a death in the family, a distant cousin perhaps, since surely any of their family in the area would have come to tell them rather than sending a note. But the paper, scented faintly of lavender, said something else entirely.

She sank onto the sofa, fingers clutching the parchment. "Miss Peverell is inviting us to dine with her and her brother?"

Her mother nodded, grey curls bobbing. "Can you imagine?"

No, she could not. Viscounts did not invite the wife and daughter of a Riding Officer to dine. More likely they might ask to see references before hiring them for some menial duty.

"I'm not sure what this means," Hester started.

Her mother clasped her hands in front of her green gown. "I know exactly what this means. Lord Peverell favors you, just as I said."

It was as if a spring breeze danced through the room, brightening, warming. Oh, traitor heart! Yet, what other explanation could there be, particularly after her challenge on the Downs on Saturday?

Rob Peverell had decided to court her.

She clutched the invitation to her chest, then lowered it and forced her voice to come out even.

"We mustn't get our hopes up, Mother. Just because he has invited us to dine does not mean anything will come of it."

"And everything might come of it," her mother insisted. She seized Hester's hands, pulling her up and crumbling the invitation in the process. "Don't you see, my girl? This could be the making of you."

Hester pulled away, leaving the parchment in her mother's hands. "I rather thought *I* was the making of me."

"You've done well," her mother assured her, smoothing the paper with her free hand. "But this? To be a viscountess? One of the highest-ranking ladies in the area? And your sister the other. Oh, I may be overcome."

She fell back on the sofa with a thump.

Hester sat beside her. "Please, Mother, do not refine on this. Now that he is the viscount, Rob Peverell is one of the most eligible bachelors in England. Dozens of ladies with impressive family lines, connections to royalty, deep dowries, and more claims to beauty than I will ever possess will be waiting to charm him."

Her mother drew herself up. "And not one of them more deserving or any better than my daughter."

Hester reached out and hugged her close. "Thank you for that. I love you, Mother."

"And I love you, darling, more than you can ever know." Her mother pulled back, smile watery. "Now, we must strategize. You'll need a new dress, new gloves. Your cloak may suffice, but perhaps new shoes as well."

Hester laughed. "Mother, if I was good enough to be invited to dinner, I see no reason to change."

"Not change," her mother said. "But presented in your best possible light." She rose. "Come with me. We must study our wardrobes, see what can be contrived. You must appear a viscountess, and I must appear the mother of one. Together, we will show Viscount Peverell and his sister just how impressive the Denbys of Upper Grace can be."

Rob had never managed a dinner party before. Well, Elizabeth was managing it, but his part was still larger than he would have thought. When his parents or brother had given a party, all he had had to do was agree to his valet's choices for evening wear, appear downstairs some time before dinner started, and smile his way through the evening before it was safe to escape to one of the gentlemen's clubs or a friendly gambling establishment.

Now, apparently, he must approve every detail, because Elizabeth kept finding him to ask his opinion.

"We didn't bring the Crown Derby from London," she announced, wandering into the study early Monday morning with two porcelain plates in her hands after he'd heard Mr. Chalder's report. The night watchman was a thick-bodied fellow with a wide nose and narrowed eyes. He seemed given to quick, simple answers, but he claimed to have seen nothing, not even Captain St. Claire.

"We have the Chelsea and the Bow," Rob's sister explained now. "Which do you think Hester would prefer?"

He couldn't imagine Hester caring about plates, but he nodded to the one with the flower and stem splayed across the glazed porcelain. "That one."

Elizabeth frowned. "Why?"

"Unless I am mistaken, that's an apple blossom. She smells like spiced apples."

Elizabeth giggled, but his answer must have satisfied her, for she wandered out.

She found him again that afternoon while he was attempting to determine which of the village plots and houses he actually owned. His father and Thomas could probably have pointed them out easily enough. He wanted to be able to do the same.

"Where shall we gather before dinner?" his sister asked, approaching the desk and cocking her head as if studying the map he'd spread out.

"Whichever room is open at the moment," Rob said, gaze returning to the colored lines.

"A useless answer."

He raised his gaze to meet hers. "Why? I thought it would be easiest for you."

"It should not be our convenience but Hester's enjoyment that should motivate us," she informed him primly. "I'm considering the third floor withdrawing room at the front of the house."

"Too many patterns," Rob complained. "The wallpaper, the carpet, those inlaid sideboards. I feel like I'm going cross-eyed every time I walk in the door."

"Perhaps Hester and her mother like patterns," she said, chin coming up. "But I could add some vases of flowers for a focal point."

"No," Rob said, straightening. "The apple blossom on the dinner plate is sufficient. I can't imagine Hester is overly fond of flowers. Her father died in a bed of them."

Elizabeth stared at him. "You're making that up."

"I wish I was," Rob told her, spreading his hands. "He was a Riding Officer who was murdered trying to stop a gang of smugglers. Hester and her sister discovered the body."

Elizabeth pressed her fingers to her chest. "How horrid. Well, no additional flowers then. Besides, I suppose it is a lot of walking to reach that one."

Relieved, Rob tried to focus on the map again.

But Elizabeth wasn't finished. "What about after dinner? Should we open the music room?"

Rob sighed. "No. We can retire to Mother's withdrawing room overlooking the Channel. Hester isn't the Queen Mother, Elizabeth."

"Well, you ought to treat her as well as the queen," she

said, but she had the good grace to leave him be until dinner.

When she laid out a dozen possibilities for the menu.

Rob was almost glad when Mercer showed up Monday afternoon with more papers and advice. At least that allowed Rob to shelter in the study. Who knew what else his sister might need his advice on? Rearranging the paintings in the family gallery to a more pleasing pattern? Fussing about whether the drapes should be opened or closed? Wondering about wood or coal for the fire? Even dealing with his persnickety steward was better than the endless questions.

"A few trivialities to tie up loose ends," Mercer assured him before pulling out a sheath of papers from his ever-present portfolio. "Leasing agreements for some of the houses and businesses in the area, the enclosure plan for the Wiltshire estate, and the like. All I require is your signature."

A few signatures would put him out of the study and into his sister's company far too soon. Rob drew the stack closer and began reading.

Mercer shifted beside him. "They are the usual sort, my lord. Nothing that need concern you."

"You are sweating, Mercer," Rob said, moving to the second page. "That alone tells me I should be concerned. Have a seat. I imagine this will take some time."

It did, but by the eighth lease affirming that so-and-so would be taking such-and-such business at this location or that for a certain amount of time for a certain amount of money, the words were beginning to run together. He moved quickly enough through the next set that he nearly missed it.

Rob frowned as he held up one of the documents. "This is a lease for my pier."

Mercer, who'd been fidgeting in his seat across the desk from Rob the entire time, stilled. "Yes, my lord, just as you requested."

"To Captain Ruggins, not Captain St. Claire."

Mercer popped to his feet. "What! Oh, that clerk. He can't get anything right. Sometimes I don't know why I consent to keep him on staff. If you would sign it, my lord, I will see to the changes."

Rob took up the quill. "No need. I'll change it myself right now." He marked out Captain Ruggins' name, added St. Claire's, initialed both changes, and signed near the bottom. "There you are. No bother."

Mercer's hand shook as he reached for the page. "How thoughtful of you, my lord."

"Give me a moment, and I'll sign the others," Rob promised. He had Mercer out of his study in a distressingly short period of time.

Elizabeth squeezed in as the steward left. "Good. You have a moment free."

"I don't know what gave you that impression," Rob said, grabbing a book and propping it open before him. "I have much to do to prepare for the next session of Parliament."

She tilted her head. "By reading *Animal Husbandry on the Scottish Moors?*"

He set down the book with a sigh. "What do you need, Elizabeth?"

"Only that you speak with Monsieur Antoine." She ventured closer. "He is being particularly difficult about the menu. Apparently, sea trout isn't in season, but I'm sure Mother served it at this time of year before."

From London, where ships brought in delicacies from around the globe on a daily basis. "I have the utmost confidence in you."

She scrunched up her face. "Please, Rob? Father used to address him when he wouldn't listen to Mother."

"It won't wash," Rob told her. "Everyone listened to Mother. We all knew she was the real power in the family."

She dropped her gaze. "Then I fear I haven't inherited her gift."

He rose and went to put an arm about her shoulders. "I know that feeling. Every day I wonder how I'll be able to take on Father's tasks."

She peered up at him through her lashes. "Then you'll speak to Monsieur Antoine?"

"Yes. This time. But if you insist on managing the staff, you will have to find a way to manage our chef as well."

Her brave smile said she would try. He headed for the kitchen.

He'd only had a few occasions to deal with their chef, notably to inform him that his position would continue now that Rob's parents were gone, but he knew the fellow's reputation. His mother had been inordinately proud of it.

"He worked in the Palace of Versailles," she'd say on the least provocation. "He served Louis himself."

"Before or after he lost his head?" Rob had quipped once.

Now he found the chef in the massive kitchen at the back of the house. The temporary staff Mrs. Catchpole in Grace-by-the-Sea had provided for the kitchen apparently included two women assistants and a scullery maid. Working with the assistant Elizabeth had brought from London, they made the chef seem the center of a whirlwind. Two fingers stroking his impressively long mustache, as black and supple as a whip, he watched every movement from his place at the head of the worktable.

"*Monsieur*," Rob called in hopes of capturing his attention.

The dark, narrowed gaze swung in his direction as the chef dropped his hand. "My lord. You are here about the meringue, *non*?"

"No," Rob allowed, venturing farther into the sunny

room. "Was there a problem with the meringue too?"

Antoine rolled his eyes heavenward as if begging the good Lord for patience. "The meringue was flat at dinner last night. I would not have served it, but your sister insisted. You have come to discharge me for the offense, *oui*?"

"No," Rob repeated. "I didn't notice, and it certainly isn't an offense worthy of discharge. Elizabeth asked me to talk to you about the menu for the dinner party tomorrow. I understand there is a problem."

He strode to the other end of the worktable, sending two of his assistants scuttling out of his way, snatched up a stained piece of parchment, and shook it at Rob. "Trout, she says. There are none. None! I have asked, I have pleaded, I have thundered! There are no sea trout in Grace-by-the-Sea."

He tried to imagine his father dealing with such vitriol and failed. Still, he was the viscount. He must maintain a calm, reasoned demeanor.

"Since there are no sea trout," Rob said, "feel free to substitute something else."

"Sub-sub-substitute?" the man sputtered, face turning a dangerous shade of red. The last assistant grabbed a mixing bowl and backed out of reach.

Antoine stalked up to Rob and shook his boney finger at him. "I do not substitute. The menu calls for sea trout, we have sea trout. The recipe asks for the piece to be served *au gratin*, it shall be served *au gratin*. Anything less is anarchy."

Rob seized the fellow's finger and held it in place. "I don't mind a little anarchy."

Antoine tried to pull back, but Rob clung fast. Such a display, however provoked, might not be worthy of his father's legacy, but it certainly felt good.

"Unhand me, sir!" the chef blustered, dark eyes beginning to look alarmed.

"When you have offered me an alternative to sea trout," Rob said pleasantly.

Antoine glared at him, as if he thought the look would set Rob's hair on fire. Rob smiled at him.

"Bass," Antoine snapped. "It is in season and plentiful, and the flavor will pair well with the lobster sauce."

Rob released him. "Excellent. Is there anything else I can do to help?"

"Get. Out. Of. My. Kitchen."

Rob made a show of glancing around. "Your kitchen. I must remember that next time I'm issuing leases. *Bon jour, monsieur.*"

He thought something slammed into the door as he shut it behind him.

"Start looking for a new chef," he told Elizabeth as he passed her in the corridor.

Her face fell. "Oh, Rob, you didn't discharge him."

"Not yet," Rob said. "But if that is any example of his behavior, I will, as soon as this dinner with Hester is over."

Because even a man like his father could be pushed too far.

CHAPTER FOURTEEN

HESTER DREW IN A DEEP breath as the Peverell coach set off for the Lodge Tuesday evening. Rob had sent the white-lacquered carriage with its gold appointments for them as if she and her mother were visiting dignitaries from a foreign country. Though her mother sat beside her on the blue velvet seat, Rebecca had reluctantly consented to remain behind.

"Just make sure you bring home a father," her daughter had said. "We could have a wedding like Aunt Rosemary's, and I could carry flowers this time."

She'd kissed Rebecca on the top of her silky hair. "Going to dinner with Lord Peverell does not mean a wedding is coming soon."

Though it certainly felt that way.

Her mother definitely thought as much. "Be sure to agree with his opinions," she advised as they started across the Downs. "Men like that."

"I suppose it doesn't matter what I like," Hester said, leaning back against the squabs with a sigh.

"Of course it matters," her mother argued. "But it will matter more after you're married."

Once she might have taken the advice. Now she knew better. She had only spent a short time with Jasper before he'd sailed off and been killed, but she understood that good marriages were made of give and take, consensus, and action. She would not be shy about telling Rob what she thought, on any subject.

The carriage rocked, and her mother frowned out at the twilight. "Wind's coming up."

Hester could see it too. The leaves she'd noticed on Saturday were flying past. Trees, bare and lonely, whipped back and forth against the sky.

Tempting to suggest that they send their regrets, but she wouldn't last another few days of her mother's fussing and her own wonderings.

A short distance from Upper Grace across the Downs, the Lodge perched atop the headland on the opposite side of Grace-by-the-Sea from Lord Howland's castle. Nestled among trees, it was a ragged outline against the darkening sky.

"Not many lamps lit," her mother commented as the coach rolled to a stop on the drive near the wide front door.

Indeed, most of the windows looked dark, the glass flickering as it reflected the torches near the front. Hester fought a shiver.

Ike Bascom, in the grey livery of the local employment agency, came out to help them alight. He offered Hester a grin before schooling his face and leading them toward the front door, even as the coach rumbled off into the twilight.

"Going to fetch the other guests," Ike said as if he'd seen Hester's look.

She glanced to her mother. "Then the Peverells are simply entertaining tonight."

Her mother lifted her chin. "So he can make a declaration in public, no doubt."

With a shake of her head, she stepped through the door Ike held open and into elegance.

The dark-wood paneling of the entry hall had been polished to such a high sheen she could see the ghost of her reflection as she moved deeper into the space. The coffered ceiling arched away above her. Was that copper between the beams? At the back of the hall, carved wood stairs led up and down into destinies unknown. The scents of lemon and lavender floated on the air.

Rob stepped from a room on the left. He'd dressed for the occasion, in a black tailcoat with velvet lapels, a white waistcoat patterned in lilies, and breeches buckled at his knees in gold. She was heartily glad her mother had insisted on wearing their finest. They hadn't had time for new gowns, but they had retrimmed the dress from Rosemary's wedding with lace and braid, and she thought she looked rather well in it.

The glow in Rob's eyes said as much.

"Mrs. Denby, Hester, welcome," he said, inclining his head so that the lamplight caught in his hair. "Would you care to join me and Elizabeth while we wait for the rest of our guests?"

He held out an arm to each of them, and her mother accepted his left with Hester on his right. Rob escorted them through a doorway that led into a gallery. They passed paintings of stern-faced gentlemen and serene ladies with hair and clothing of long ago before entering a withdrawing room with walls the color of persimmons. Gilt-edged panels framed paintings of hunting dogs, horses, and landscapes of the Downs.

Elizabeth, gowned in grey, was perched on a sofa with gold tassels along the edges. She patted the seat beside her. "Hester, dear, come sit with me. Mrs. Denby, I know you will favor the chair just there. I'm delighted you could join us."

Hester went to sit, glad for her mother at her elbow on a satin-striped chair with lions leering from the arms. "I understand you are expecting others."

"Yes," Elizabeth said brightly. "Lord Featherstone and Mr. Donner from the spa will be dining with us this evening."

"Even numbers," her mother muttered.

Hester knew the custom, though she had never felt bound by it. Then again, any special dinners at their house were generally reserved for family.

"Have you visited the Lodge before, Mrs. Denby?" Elizabeth asked as Rob leaned against the white marble hearth. Hester fought to keep her gaze on their hostess.

"I haven't had the opportunity," her mother admitted. "It seems grander than I expected."

"That's because we are showing you our finest tonight," Elizabeth assured her. She turned to her brother. "We have time. Why don't we give Hester and her mother a more thorough tour?"

Rob eyed his sister. "Are you certain? The whole place is something of a maze, and we've only opened a handful of rooms for our stay this time."

That sounded far too cautious for him. It was almost as if he thought his home wasn't good enough for her.

"I wouldn't mind a tour," Hester put in.

Rob opened his mouth as if to protest further, but Elizabeth jumped in. "Excellent. I'll just wait here for the other guests. I'm sure you can manage, Brother."

Rob closed his mouth as if resigned and straightened away from the hearth. Hester rose, but her mother leaned back in her chair.

"Why, I would never be so unkind as to leave you, Miss Peverell. You go ahead, Hester."

"Colluding," Rob murmured as he moved to join Hester.

With a frown to her mother, she took his arm and let him lead her from the room.

"Do you not tire of the manipulations?" she asked as they ventured back down the long gallery.

"When it affords me a moment alone with you?" Rob asked. "Certainly not. I should thank your mother."

Hester glanced back and spotted her mother and his sister craning their necks to watch. Catching her gaze, they quickly busied themselves in conversation.

"It is only a tour," Hester said, returning her gaze to Rob. "Perhaps you could start by explaining more about these fine ladies and gentlemen on the wall."

He stopped in front of a painting of a woman sitting in a high-backed chair, surrounded by three children of various ages. The lady's hair was the color of Elizabeth's, and her charming smile reminded Hester of Rob's. The children appeared to adore her. The oldest boy, standing on one side, had his hand on her shoulder, expression serious, and the sunny-faced little girl in muslin at her right knee beamed up at her. Another boy stood at her left knee, but he looked out into the world, hazel gaze curiously vacant.

"This," Rob said, "is my mother and her children."

Hester frowned. "I recognize Elizabeth, and the older boy must be your brother, Thomas. If that last child is you, you must have changed a great deal as you grew."

"Less than you might think," he said. "At least, in demeanor. I found it difficult to stand still for the hours required for a proper portrait. Mother excused me. The painter finished my part of the piece from memory."

"Then I must question his memory," Hester said, privately wondering why Rob alone would be excused. "Though I suppose now that you're the viscount, you can have your own portrait painted."

He cut her a glance. "Perhaps when I have my viscountess beside me."

Her cheeks were warming as she and Rob came out into the entry hall, where Ike was on duty. Seeing them, he snapped to attention.

"Now, what else can I show you of my monstrosity of a house?" Rob asked her. "My steward tells me we may have foundation issues in the crooked wing, so we should likely avoid that."

Though Ike likely should be pretending he wasn't listening, he nodded as if agreeing.

"Crooked wing?" Hester couldn't help asking.

"The main block of the house, where we stand now, was built in the seventeenth century," he explained. "Subsequent viscounts added a wing to the east and one to the west as well as an addition for a larger kitchen and more room for the servants. My grandfather contributed another wing that juts out from the southwest corner at a forty-five-degree angle. My parents, Thomas, and my steward call it the rear wing. Elizabeth named it the crooked wing when she was younger. The appellation suits the place."

That sounded like a great deal of house. Hester glanced up the stairs. "Perhaps you could show me your favorite room."

He nodded. "This way, then."

They climbed to the next story, and he led her into another withdrawing room, where the lamps remained lit and a cheery fire warmed the white marble hearth. Unlike the one where Elizabeth had greeted her, this one had cool green walls and deeper green velvet drapes on either side of a bank of windows looking out into the night.

"The house includes three withdrawing rooms," he told Hester, venturing deeper into the room. "This was my mother's favorite. I sometimes feel as if she's still here."

"You were close to your mother too, then?" Hester asked, daring to put a finger to the Dresden porcelain shepherdess standing guard on a table near the striped sofa.

"Reasonably," he said, leaning his hip against the sofa's back where it bisected the space. "I didn't share all my escapades with her, but she knew enough to chide me on occasion. She always urged me to find a purpose. I doubt she expected that purpose to be taking over Father's responsibilities, and hers."

His gaze was on the flat of the sofa, head cocked as if he imagined his mother seated there. "And if you hadn't been elevated to viscount, what then? What did you expect your purpose to be?"

He glanced up at her, brow furrowed. "I hadn't decided. The church seemed far too tame, the military too dangerous. In my heart, I knew I couldn't continue as I was, but nothing more beckoned."

"I know the feeling," Hester confessed. "I always thought to be a wife and mother. I am a mother, though no longer a wife. I love teaching, but I ask myself what else might be in my future."

"That's it exactly." He straightened away from the sofa. "I suppose I'll never know now. My fate is sealed. Viscount Peverell."

He said the word as if it tasted foul.

"Surely being a viscount isn't so bad," Hester commiserated. "You have Elizabeth. You have all this."

"And two hundred people awaiting my every decision," he reminded her.

"I'm sure they are capable of making a few decisions on their own," she countered.

He sighed. "I hope so, for I'm not sure of the decisions I'm making." He shifted on his feet. "How did you do it, Hester? How did you move beyond the tragedies—your father's death, your husband's?"

Hester shrugged. "I suppose I just did what must be done."

"Fortitude," he said. "The ability to rise above life's challenges."

She could not see herself as so noble. "It wasn't as if I had the luxury of choice."

"Neither do I," he said.

Hester rallied. "You have choices. You can choose

where to live, how to use your income for the good of others. Look what you did for our school."

"A whim," he confessed. "I was hoping to impress you."

She almost slipped into his earnest gaze. "You have, Rob."

He leaned closer, and all at once his lips were brushing hers again, softly gently, there and gone, like the sweetest of dreams.

From downstairs came the sound of voices. The time for confidences had passed. She stepped back from him.

He moved around the sofa. "Unless I miss my guess, the others have arrived. Shall we?" He offered her his arm.

Hester accepted it and accompanied him toward the door, but she was certain their conversation, and his kiss, would stay with her for some time to come.

How fine to have a moment for just the two of them. That she'd allowed his kiss said she'd forgiven him for his lack of response on the Downs. Elizabeth had said this party would allow him to see how Hester fit into their world. He would not be able to enter his mother's withdrawing room without seeing Hester there as well. With great reluctance, he returned her to the formal withdrawing room, where Elizabeth had decided to welcome everyone.

Lord Featherstone and Donner had arrived, and greetings were exchanged all around. Like Rob, the baron was dressed in his evening black, satin lapels catching the light as he bowed over Mrs. Denby's hand.

Donner was in grey, white breeches buckled at the knee in silver and a cravat with a fold far more complicated than Rob's valet had ever attempted. Rob watched his sister as Donner greeted her, but Elizabeth's smile seemed no brighter than it had been when she'd welcomed Hester and her mother. Certainly, she and Donner gave off no sparks of interest.

Unlike him and Hester.

Whoever spoke as they all sat conversing, whatever was said, his attentions kept coming back to her. The way she smiled when her mother mentioned Rebecca. The way her fingers tucked back a honey-thick curl behind one ear, making him wish he'd been the one to do so. Her sweet laugh at a quip from Lord Featherstone, raising his smile as well.

He'd told her things on their short tour he'd never intended to share with another soul, and it felt right. As if they had found their way back to each other.

It was a good thing they only had a short time to converse before Bascom came to announce that dinner was ready to be served, or Rob might have found a way to kiss her again.

As it was, he made sure to offer his arm to her before Lord Featherstone could beat him to it. "Mrs. Todd, if I may?"

She tucked her hand in his elbow. "Delighted, my lord."

Behind them, he heard the baron offering to escort her mother and Donner asking after Elizabeth.

"Very clever of your sister," Hester whispered as Rob led her back down the gallery for the entry hall. "A gentleman for each lady."

He grinned at her. "The *right* gentleman for each lady."

Her cheeks turned pink.

He led them all down the staircase to the ground floor dining room. Elizabeth was right to call it cavernous. Here too, the walls were paneled in squares of wood, but the floor was flagstone, and the dining table could easily seat twenty. A more intimate number of place settings had been gathered at one end. Glass-paned doors at the other end of the room led out into the rear yard.

Going to the head of the table, Rob pulled out the chair on his right for Hester. Elizabeth took the chair on his left, with Donner beside her. Lord Featherstone and Mrs. Denby joined Hester on the right.

"Will you say the grace, Brother?" Elizabeth asked.

Rob blinked a moment, surprised by the request. All his guests waited expectantly. Well, he'd been speaking more often to his Lord lately. Why not now?

He bowed his head. "Dear Lord, we thank You for such warm friendships on a cold night, for good food from Your bounty, and for the many hands that grew it and will serve it to us. Most of all, we thank You for your gracious blessings. Amen."

Amens echoed down the table, but he caught Hester gazing at him as if surprised he even knew how to pray. He could have told her it was a skill recently acquired, if heartfelt.

He tried to maintain that sense of thankfulness and good cheer as the dinner progressed. In such company, however, it was easy to fall back on his old ways. A tease here, a story there, and he soon had his guests laughing. Monsieur Antoine must have found his bass, even if he'd smothered it in a succulent lobster sauce. He'd accompanied it with potatoes *au gratin* and a medley of autumn vegetables Rob could only compliment.

Mrs. Denby must have felt the same way. "I must ask your chef for this recipe, Miss Peverell," she said, fork lifting a bite of the fish. "It's delightful."

"Monsieur Antoine is very talented," Elizabeth agreed.

And still employed. Rob allowed himself a little smile.

"Do you like the recipe?" Hester asked beside him.

"It's delicious," he admitted. "It just gives me a great deal of food for thought."

She laughed at the pun.

The glass-paned doors rattled. Rob's head came up. Everyone stilled, gazes going in that direction.

"Is someone outside?" Mrs. Denby asked, brow puckered.

In the act of serving the next course, Bascom looked to Rob as if asking whether he should go check.

"No," Rob assured everyone a moment before the doors banged open and the wind rushed into the room.

CHAPTER FIFTEEN

R OB WAS ON HIS FEET before Bascom could react. The footman scurried to match his stride as he moved down the table against a wind that drove raindrops like icy spears into the room. Together, they managed to close the doors. Light spilling through the glass showed Rob the shrubs on the back lawn shaking with the wind, while rain set about flattening the last flowers.

"Sorry, my lord," Bascom murmured. "I checked it last night on my rounds to close the house. I thought it was securely latched."

"It's latched now," Rob told him. Turning, he smiled at his guests, most of whom were on their feet and staring at the doors. "A little excitement to whet the appetite for dessert. I believe you wanted to serve it in the upper withdrawing room, Elizabeth."

Her sister gathered her composure. "Yes, thank you, Rob. Ladies, will you join me?"

Hester and her mother followed her up the stairs. Bascom made for the door to the kitchen, likely to fetch the others to come clear the table.

"I'd be delighted to drink port with you and reminisce about wars we never fought, gentlemen," Rob said, coming back to the table and flicking drops of rain off his coat. "But I think you will find the evening much improved if we join the ladies now."

"You have no need to convince me, sir," Lord Feather-stone said. He had been the only one not to leap to his feet. He rose now and came to clap Rob on his shoulder. "I'm sure this night will be remembered for more than the wind at the door."

He started up the stairs.

Donner moved to Rob's side. "No sign of a ship?"

"I can't see the Channel in the dark, but on a night like tonight?" Rob shook his head. "Any captain worth his salt will know not to set out or come in when the wind's up like this. That's when wrecks happen. So, you have no reason to ply your trade either, Donner."

With a rueful smile, he accompanied Rob up the stairs.

Elizabeth had arranged for tea and a selection of biscuits to be served in their mother's withdrawing room. Bascom brought in the tray shortly after they were all seated. The drapes had been closed over the windows that looked out on the Channel, but that didn't stop Donner from taking a peek into the night. He shook his head at Rob as he returned to the group.

"I haven't ever visited during the autumn before," Elizabeth confessed as she doled out teacups with the amber brew. "Is this sort of thing usual?"

"We do get our occasional storms," Hester's mother allowed.

"Mrs. Tully would probably have a tale about the gale of '98 or some such," Hester agreed with a fond smile. "I shouldn't expect it to last long."

But as they talked, Rob could hear the rising noise, the shudder that went through the house at a particularly hard gust. The fire was gutting in the hearth, and the chimney let out a moan, as if it too bore the brunt of the storm.

"That sounds serious," Lord Featherstone said, setting down his cup. "We may have to cut short our time with you, Miss Peverell, to ensure our own safety returning to the village."

Elizabeth glanced toward Donner. "Oh, must you?"

"Bascom," Rob called, and the young footman stepped closer, brows up in question. "Would you ask Mr. Fitch his thoughts?"

"Right away, my lord." He hurried from the room.

"The Downs should be fine," Mrs. Denby said to no one in particular. "There are few trees to blow across the road."

"But a fine fetch to build up a wind," Lord Featherstone argued. "I've heard it can sweep through with the force of an Indian hurricane."

"Well, you are all welcome to spend the night," Elizabeth said. "We have plenty of rooms."

Spend the night, with Hester just down the corridor? How easy to slip to her chamber, offer to comfort her. He could take her in his arms and kiss the fear from her face. Who knew where such intimacies might lead?

He knew. Such intimacies had been inappropriate the summer they'd first met and were even more so now. He would do nothing that might cause her dishonor.

"Surely it won't come to that," Hester said as if she had heard his thoughts. "Your coachman seems quite skilled, and he must know these roads well by now."

But when Bascom returned a few moments later, it seemed she was wrong.

"Mr. Fitch is concerned, my lord," he reported. "If he could stay on the headland, he might have no trouble, but he has to cross the Downs to reach either Upper Grace or Grace-by-the-Sea. He's worried the coach could overturn by accident."

Both Hester and her mother shuddered at that. He could understand why. He'd had enough taken from him by an accident.

"Then it's settled," he said. "Bascom, tell Mr. Fitch there will be no more travels tonight. I trust the stables and coach house are secure."

"They seemed solid as a rock, my lord," Bascom said.

"Good. Off you go, then." As the footman strode from the room, Rob turned to his sister. "Elizabeth, I'll need your help to determine how many of Mrs. Catchpole's staff are still in the Lodge and where we can house them tonight. We'll need them to set up rooms for our guests as well."

She rose. "Of course. Mr. Donner, perhaps you could assist me."

"At your side," Donner vowed.

"I'd like to help as well," Hester put in as Rob narrowed his eyes at the two leaving the room.

He looked to her. "Excellent. I propose a treasure hunt."

Lord Featherstone and her mother stood.

"A treasure hunt?" Mrs. Denby asked.

"You may have noticed that this house spreads in multiple directions," Rob explained. "We'll need to find four bedchambers, preferably close together so staff can be available should anyone need assistance during the night."

"I'd suggest two bedchambers, with large beds," Lord Featherstone put in. "The temperature will likely drop tonight, and it wouldn't be right to ask anyone to venture to the coal shed in this weather. The fewer fires needed, the better."

"Excellent thought," Rob agreed. "Two bedchambers, then: one for you and Donner, one for Mrs. Denby and Mrs. Todd."

And that ought to keep any amorous wanderings at a minimum, for either Donner or him.

A treasure hunt, he called it. Hester shook her head but took the candelabra Rob lighted and followed him from

the withdrawing room. Her mother and Lord Featherstone came behind with their own light.

"The first floor holds mostly function rooms," Rob
explained as they gathered by the stairs. "Among them,
the withdrawing room and gallery you saw, a library, a
study, and an exercise room that stretches over most of
one wing."

"I take it your forebears were particularly manly," Lord
Featherstone mused with a smile.

"Fencing, pugilism, even some Eastern art that involved
using your feet," Rob agreed. "My brother Thomas was a
devotee. Give me a good pistol and a knife."

Hester could imagine him facing down an opponent,
knife between his teeth.

"Unfortunately, none of those rooms will do for our
purposes," he continued. "This floor isn't much use
either, which leaves the third story, where we generally
housed our guests. I propose Mrs. Todd and I take the
west wing, and Mrs. Denby and Lord Featherstone take
the east. We'll report back at the stairs in a half hour. All
agreed?"

Her mother and Lord Featherstone nodded, but Hester
couldn't help the chill that went through her. "Are you
certain there isn't a way for us to return home? Rebecca
will be frightened."

Her mother touched her hand. "We must rely on Nurse
Peters. She won't fail us."

"And I will do my utmost not to fail you," Rob promised.

By the determined look on his face, she could believe
that.

They started up the stairs. Shadows danced away from
the lamps, but darkness was never far distant. To make
matters worse, the wind whistled through windows,
howled down chimneys. And the entire floor creaked as
if an army were sneaking up on them.

Hester found herself walking closer to Rob as they separated from her mother and Lord Featherstone and headed down the west wing. The dark paneling swallowed the light and the thick carpet muffled their steps. If her hands hadn't been braced on the candelabra, she knew she would have reached for him.

Instead, she tried to focus on their task. "How many rooms are there, all told?" she asked him as he paused to open a door.

"Somewhere between thirty and forty," he said, lifting his lamp to reveal furniture shrouded in Holland covers, as if sheep squatted on the fine carpet. "Depending on whether you count dressing rooms and quarters for the servants. Elizabeth and I tried to count the rooms once. We got rather muddled and had to shout for someone to come find us."

"You're teasing me," she accused as he glanced around.

"No, indeed," he vowed. "As I recall, an elderly fellow in doublet and hose located us and directed us back to our parents. He bore a strong resemblance to the first Viscount Peverell. We never found him again either. He's probably still wandering the halls from the last masquerade."

Hester swatted his arm with her free hand, and the candelabra wavered. Their shadows climbed the walls like gnarled vines. Her laughter stuck in her throat.

"I don't believe in ghosts," Rob said, perhaps a little louder than was needed. "This is my home, for all it can be a nuisance. It seems someone saw fit to pillage this room of a large-enough bed for two. Let's try the next room."

They tried the next several on that side, then circled back on the other. All were well secured for a long absence—no sheets, no coverlets. Some lacked beds or had ones that were not conducive to sharing. Two whistled so loudly with the wind that no one would have slept a wink.

Rob shook his head as they started back for the main block of the house to meet her mother and Lord Featherstone. "What did I expect? Father hasn't visited in years. We probably haven't hosted a house party in a decade. It seems the Lodge has fallen to ruin."

He sounded so sad, as if he were guilty of some great dearth of duty. "Not to ruin," Hester told him. "A few more staff, a good cleaning, and all should be well."

"I would not be so certain of that, Mrs. Todd," Lord Featherstone said, materializing out of the darkness with her mother at his side. "I fear we found that the roof has been leaking on this wing, my lord. Many of the furnishings and carpets will require replacing."

Rob's sigh was audible. "Thank you for the report, my lord. I am dismayed to hear it, but I will do what I can to remedy the matter once this storm abates. In the meantime…" He turned and gazed back the way they had come. "It appears we must attempt the crooked wing after all."

Rob hadn't wandered the crooked wing in years. He couldn't help wrinkling his nose at the musty, unused smell as they all reached the carpeted corridor.

"We'll take the left if you and Mrs. Denby take the right," he advised the baron.

"Very good." Lord Featherstone led Hester's mother toward the closest door on that side just as a cracking noise echoed down the corridor. Rob would have sworn the entire wing canted to the right. Hester clutched his arm.

Rob put his hand over hers. "Some version of this house has stood on the promontory for more than a hundred and fifty years. I doubt one storm will sweep it away."

She offered him a game smile. "Of course. Please forgive me."

"Nothing to forgive. It is an impressive storm. There's something about wind—the speed, the force, the way it spears through the least crack. It's not so noticeable in London, but here? We are witness to the power of nature."

"You almost sound as if you enjoy it," she accused as he opened the door and they peered into the room.

"Perhaps a bit," he admitted. "You can't deny there's an excitement to the air."

"Not everyone loves excitement the way you do," she informed him. She removed her hand from his arm to step into the room. "This one isn't so bad. A large enough bed to share. Few Holland covers to remove."

"Father favored this room," Rob said, following her. "He'd engage Mother or Thomas in a game of chess on that table there by the hearth."

The round ebony table was inlaid with ivory to mark the squares for the game. He could almost see his father rubbing his hands together gleefully before pronouncing check and mate. Chess had been an active sport for his father. He'd loved the strategy, but he'd seemed to love knocking over his opponent's king far more, as if the clack of ivory meeting ebony gave him a peculiar pleasure.

"Is your mother's room next door, then?" Hester asked, turning from the big box bed.

"Down the corridor. There are two large dressing rooms in between."

"Could we use those for the staff?" she asked.

Rob stuck out his lower lip. "Possibly. I seem to recall cots that could be brought in when Mother or Father was ailing and needed a servant close at hand. The question would be where those cots were stored. Our housekeeper would be able to put her hands on them, but we left her in London this time."

She came to join him by the hearth. "How odd not to know your own home."

He felt it too, as if the place hadn't really been home until Hester had come to stand next to him. "You forget," he told her. "We only stayed here during the summers, and Mother made all the arrangements. Elizabeth even had to order in coal for this visit. We probably should have stayed in London, but the house there and the estate in Wiltshire hold too many memories. I thought it would be easier for me and Elizabeth here for a time. Yet it seems ghosts followed us, for I see Mother, Father, and Thomas everywhere."

She raised her chin. "Then we should not use this room. Let's look farther down the corridor."

In the end, they decided on guest rooms across from each other just down the wing. Rob left Hester, her mother, and Lord Featherstone to start setting the rooms to rights and went in search of his sister. Elizabeth and Donner were returning from the kitchen, along with several of the maids and Bascom, all armed with sheets, blankets, and coal.

It took a while to settle everyone. Elizabeth loaned nightgowns to Hester and her mother and Rob found nightshirts for Donner and Lord Featherstone. His sister returned to her room, but Rob knew he wouldn't be able to shut his eyes. The wind moaned down the corridors, and the house shuddered at random moments. Something crashed from the back of the house—a tree going down, perhaps? And he couldn't stop thinking about the rainwater that must be pouring into the east wing.

He'd asked Bascom to keep lamps burning in the corridors and stairwell in case anyone needed to move in the night, so it was easy to see his way to the stairs. A shadow passed on the landing below. Rob tensed.

"Who's there?" he demanded.

Bascom climbed to his side. "Only me, my lord. I thought it best to keep an eye on the house tonight."

"Did you, now."

His tone must have sounded as suspicious as he felt, for Bascom shuffled his feet.

"That's what footmen do, isn't it?" he asked plaintively. "If I've given some offense, my lord, I wish you would tell me. I promise you, I'll rectify the matter."

Rob regarded him a moment. That brown hair hung down over a forehead too furrowed for a youth. He was carrying a heavy burden as well.

"Why did you become a footman, Bascom?" he asked.

"My mum was in service," the boy replied, chin coming up just the slightest. "She kept the castle clean when the Howlands weren't in residence. She seemed content doing the work, and it was steady. And most folks around here aren't eager to trust me, after what my father did."

"Smuggling," Rob said.

He nodded. "Just so, my lord. I worked for Captain St. Claire for a time, but his jobs aren't steady either."

So there was a connection between those two as well. "Not such a good smuggler, then," Rob observed, watching him.

Bascom's head snapped up. "Captain St. Claire isn't a smuggler, my lord. He's a, that is he works for, well he has important things that need doing. Just not often enough for me. So, I asked Mrs. Catchpole whether she could find me a place. I thought if I impressed a visitor, he might take me off with him when he left." He glanced at Rob.

The fellow couldn't know how much, and how little, he'd confessed. "I can't promise you further work, Bascom. That will be up to my sister. But I will be sure she knows how hard you're trying."

"Thank you, my lord," he said with a grateful sigh.

"You check the lower floors," Rob said. "I'll check the upper."

Bascom hesitated for just a moment, then nodded. "Very good, my lord." He headed back down the stairs.

Rob climbed to the third story and followed the west wing to the end, mind sorting through possibilities. Could Bascom still be in league with smugglers? He'd had no choice in his father's vocation, but he certainly hadn't had to throw in his lot with St. Claire. And what was that muttered business about what St. Claire was really doing out on the Channel?

He paused at the end of the wing. The window there was lashed by rain, the drops melting down the glass like quicksilver. He touched the pane, and cold seeped into his fingers. Squinting, he made out the shapes of the nearest trees, gaunt against a smoke-colored sky, whipping back and forth.

He started down the crooked wing. The moaning was worse here because of the hollow space of a ballroom below, yet he was certain he heard someone snoring. Lord Featherstone perhaps? Or Donner. He grinned imagining his sister's face when he informed her that her sweetheart sounded like a herd of cattle lowing.

In a moment between breath and moan, another sound whispered. Sobbing?

It seemed to be coming from the room where Hester and her mother were to sleep. Though he had promised himself he would not disturb her, nothing could have stopped him from easing open the door and peering inside.

Hester had been sitting on one of the upholstered chairs near the hearth, head in her hands. Her hair was down around her shoulders and glowing gold in the light of the coals. As the gleam from the corridor trickled into the room, she popped to her feet to fly to him.

"Oh, Rob, I've been so scared! Don't leave me!"

"Never," Rob vowed, folding her closer. Her spiced apple scent surrounded him; her trembling body warmed against his.

Oh, but his good intentions were being tested!

CHAPTER SIXTEEN

ROB'S ARM PRESSED HESTER CLOSE. His body, so firm and strong, warmed her through the nightgown. For a moment, she rested her head against his shoulder and just allowed herself to feel safe, protected, and cherished.

"There, now," he murmured. "What frightened you so?"

"I heard a noise," she admitted, pausing to inhale the spice of his cologne. "A terrible crash. I thought the roof might be peeling off."

"I've seen no sign of that, thank the good Lord," he told her. "The house seems to be holding together."

As if to disagree with him, cracks and pops echoed down the corridor.

She burrowed closer. "I don't remember anything this fierce. How can the others sleep?"

He turned his head, as if eyeing her mother on the tester bed. "I don't know. I certainly couldn't close my eyes."

Neither could she, or only for a moment. With the strange house, the odd noises, concern for her daughter, and everything that had happened at the dinner party, her mind was teeming.

He shifted, and all at once she was aware of how near they stood. She pulled herself out of his embrace and smoothed down the nightgown.

"What are you doing here?" she asked.

She thought she heard a chuckle over the whistle of the wind. "Afraid I make a habit of strolling into a lady guest's bedchamber?"

Her cheeks grew quite warm indeed. Mindful of her mother, she pushed him out of the room and shut the door behind her.

"*Do* you make a habit of it?" she challenged.

In the lamp-lit corridor, she could see him clearly. That hair was even more tousled than usual. Her fingers positively itched to thread their way through it.

"No, alas," he answered her with a rueful face. "Father wasn't invited to house parties of that sort. And he wouldn't have allowed me to attend others like it if I had been invited."

Easy enough to say. "But there will be ladies waiting for you in London," Hester guessed.

"Not waiting," he insisted. "Lying in wait more like. Young, virile, wealthy, charming viscounts are in high demand, you know."

Hester hid her smile. "Then you certainly don't need me to fawn over you. Or them either, I imagine. You do it quite well enough on your own."

"A palpable hit," he said, touching his hand to his heart as if she had wounded him. "I could wish that you looked on me kindly, and not because you're frightened by the wind."

He looked so contrite, so proper, yet she could not forget the way he'd held her, as if she meant everything to him.

"Why did you invite me to dinner?" she asked.

He shrugged. "I'm told that's what a gentleman does when he's interested in furthering his acquaintance with a lady."

"Furthering my acquaintance?" She was surprised how inadequate that sounded. "Then we remain merely friends."

He leaned closer, hazel eyes darkening. "Oh, Hester, I would like us to be so much more than friends, but I don't think now is the best time to discuss it."

With him looking at her that way, her standing in nothing but his sister's nightgown, most likely not. Yet she needed to know.

"Now seems perfect to me," she informed him. "There's no one about to overhear. And neither of us appears to be sleeping."

Below them came a crash that rattled against her toes.

She gasped. "What was that?"

His arms tightened just the slightest. "Have no concerns, Hester. I'll see to the matter."

He sounded so noble. It wasn't hard to imagine him a valiant knight marching the halls to keep them all safe. But her hands reached out and clung to his arm.

"You promised not to leave me," she reminded him.

He regarded her a moment, then nodded. "Come along, then. Let's see what we can learn."

"Let me fetch a blanket," Hester said.

The few moments it took to find one of the extra blankets his staff had left her and her mother was enough for her to argue with herself. Walking the house in a nightgown with a gentleman? What was she thinking?

Well, she wasn't likely to fall asleep for a while, and making sure the house was safe was at least a useful way to occupy her time and calm some of her fears.

And it wasn't really a nightgown any longer. The thick wool blanket hid her curves as effectively as a winter cloak.

And it wasn't a gentleman. It was Rob.

That alone made her consider staying in the room.

In the end, she joined him in the corridor in her stockinged feet, and they set out to the tune of snoring so fierce it almost drowned out the wind. She would not have thought it of the thoroughly refined Lord Featherstone.

The air swirling down the corridor set the lamps to sputtering against the dark-paneled walls, and the carpet was cold against her toes. Hester tucked the blanket closer. For once, Rob did not seem disposed to talk.

"You haven't answered my question," she pointed out.

He shot her a quick smile. "Sorry. I find myself thinking about the east wing. I can barely manage my staff. How am I to choose furnishings, wallpaper?"

"That shouldn't be so hard," Hester said. "Your mother's withdrawing room is beautiful. She obviously had excellent taste. Copy it, and perhaps add a special touch to each room to make it unique—an inlaid chess board like the one in your father's room, one of Abigail Bennett's landscapes."

Again he glanced her way. "Perhaps you could advise me."

Pleasure warmed her more than the blanket. "I'd be delighted."

They were nearing the end of the corridor and the window overlooking the Channel. Hester became aware of another noise—a rhythmic crash and roar.

"Is that the waves?" she asked.

Rob nodded. "The storm must be forcing them against the cliff."

She could only hope they would not reach so high as the house.

Just then, something flashed from the window. Thunder followed—deep and long—until the house reverberated with it.

"Nothing like a good lightning storm," Rob said rather gleefully when it quieted again.

"If you say it's exciting, I will scream," Hester vowed.

He chuckled. "Very well. I won't say it. But we both know I'm thinking it."

The lightning flashed again. This time she saw the zagged bolt plunge for the sea, illuminating all around it. As the light faded, Rob frowned.

"Was that a ship off the promontory?" Hester asked, blinking away the brightness.

"If it was, it won't come in," he predicted. "Such a driving tide would force any ship against the cliff. But at least the light showed me the reason for the crash we heard. A tree's come down near the entrance to the ballroom. We'll see to it in the morning. Let's get you back to bed."

It was an abrupt end to their walk, but he was right. They had solved the mystery of the crash. Still, she stayed close to his side as they started back to her room. The thunder rumbled through the house again, setting her to shivering. She clutched the blanket tight.

"Rebecca hates thunder," she said as they neared her door. "She says it makes her feel small."

"It makes all of us feel small," Rob said, stopping before her door. "I had no idea this storm was coming, but I'm sorry for separating you from your daughter at a time like this, Hester. I promise you, we'll go to her as soon as the roads allow in the morning."

She would have to take solace in that.

He glanced both ways along the corridor as she put her hand on the door.

"I'm not sure this walk was any help," he said. "A nocturnal stroll through haunted corridors isn't conducive to a good night's sleep."

"I thought you didn't believe in ghosts," she teased.

He snorted. "Only the ghosts of my past, which seem determined to sneak up on me."

"They have no call," she said. "You've changed, Rob. I can see it. You're steadier now, more dependable. You have proven others can count on you, that you will be there, come what may."

His gaze fell on her, full and sure. "I left you before,

Hester, without a backward glance. But I promise you, I've thought on that summer so many times over the years, wishing things had ended differently. Thank you for this second chance."

A second chance. A hope for a future. "I'm glad you wanted to further my acquaintance," she murmured.

Once more he bent and brushed her cheek with his lips. It was far from the first time he'd stolen a kiss, but the touch shook her.

"Good night, Hester," he said as he straightened.

Heart full, she nodded. "Good night, Rob."

As soon as the door shut behind Hester, Rob turned and strode across the corridor to rap on the door of the room Donner and Lord Featherstone were sharing. The snoring shut off immediately. A moment later, and Donner answered his knock.

"My lord?" he asked with a frown.

"There's a ship off the headland," Rob said. "The captain may be the fellow you've been seeking. I don't know whether he'll attempt to come in when the storm has passed, but get dressed, and keep watch with me."

"At once," Donner promised.

Rob paced up and down, pausing only a moment to listen. The house had gone silent, as if everything had suddenly fallen asleep. Was the storm over, then? Or merely gathering strength before pounding the promontory anew?

Donner opened the door again, now fully dressed. So was the older baron at his side.

"Donner tells me we may have trouble," Lord Featherstone said as they stepped out into the corridor. "How might I be of assistance?"

"Smugglers may be coming in," Rob advised. "Though it's possible the storm drove them off course from some other landing along the coast, and they'll return to it instead."

"But you suspect they intend to land at the Lodge," Donner said, as if hoping that would be the case.

Rob nodded. "And be warned that I am unsure of my footman, Bascom. He may be involved. We must rely only on ourselves."

Together, they moved down the corridor for the stairs. The lamplight cast a golden glow, but a dozen brigands could have been hiding in the shadows. Donner kept glancing around as if he feared as much.

"I'd like to check each external door and the windows on the ground floor," Rob told his tense companions. "Then we'll watch from the green withdrawing room to see what that ship does."

"Should we notify the authorities?" Lord Featherstone asked as they started down the stairs.

Donner cast Rob a look and shook his head. He needn't have worried that Rob was about to betray the fellow's doubts concerning the magistrate.

"I fear no one could come to our aid in the middle of this storm," he told them both. "Nor could my staff reach the village safely to request assistance. We must defend ourselves, if it comes to that."

They reached the entry hall without seeing another soul. Rob rattled the latches on the front door.

"Locked," he reported. "The other entrances are on the lower level."

Donner and the baron followed as he continued down the stairs for the ground floor. Where was Bascom? Surely he hadn't gone outside in the storm to signal the ship. Yet why hadn't he checked in with Rob again? Didn't he hear Rob and his companions wandering about? It was as if he, Donner, and Lord Featherstone were the only people in all the sprawling manor house.

They reached the ground floor and the dining room. A single candle still burned, leaving most of the long room nothing but a hollow of darkness.

"I latched the doors to the rear yard myself after they blew open at dinner," Rob said. "But we'd be remiss not to confirm they're still secured."

"Allow me." Donner pushed past Rob to head down the table. A thump and a muffled oath told him the intelligence agent had collided with something in the dark. Then he heard the latches clicking.

"Locked," Donner called. "But I can see a bit of yard through the glass. You're right—tree limbs and debris everywhere. Wait. Someone's out there!"

Rob seized one of the silver candelabra from the table and weighed it in his hand. "That ought to dent a head nicely."

"Indeed," Lord Featherstone said, taking up the other candelabra in one hand and the lit candle in the other. Together, they advanced toward the door. Rob raised the candelabra like a club and nodded to Donner, who flung open the door, splashing rain all about.

"Who's there?" Rob demanded. "Show yourself."

His watchman, Mr. Chalder, stepped into the light, wrinkled face slick with water. Rain streamed down from the cap on his head and darkened the shoulders of his wool coat. It gleamed on his boots where the black leather wasn't crusted with mud and leaves.

"Sorry, my lord," he said, lowering his head as if ashamed as water dripped from his lips. "It's not a fit night for man nor beast, but I thought I should do my duty."

Rob lowered the silver. "I applaud you for your tenacity. Why don't you come inside for now?"

Again, he bobbed his head. "Thank you, my lord."

Feeling foolish, Rob ducked back into the dining room. Donner, Lord Featherstone, and Chalder followed.

"The fire in the kitchen should only be banked," Rob advised the watchman, tipping his head toward the servant's door to the kitchen addition. "Stoke it up, and dry yourself off. If anyone gives you trouble, tell them to find me. And make sure the kitchen door is secured."

"Yes, my lord." He shuffled over to the door and disappeared down the short corridor.

Rob and Lord Featherstone returned the candelabra to their places on the long table, then retreated with Donner to the withdrawing room overlooking the Channel, stopping only long enough to retrieve a spyglass from the study. For the next few hours, the three of them took turns peering out, as the view turned from black to a smudged grey with a rising moon. The last of the storm scurried across the sea toward France. The trees stopped their frantic dancing. All grew still again.

Donner drew in a deep breath and lowered the glass to hand it to Rob. "It seems the Lodge will survive, my lord."

"In some shape," Lord Featherstone agreed, standing by the window and gazing down at the debris-cluttered yard.

"I'll have to see to the east wing," Rob acknowledged, squinting through the eyepiece. The waves came into view, still choppy and capped in silver in the moonlight. They splashed against the bow of the sailing ship that had appeared around the headland.

Was someone heading for his pier after all?

CHAPTER SEVENTEEN

HESTER WASN'T SURE SHE'D SLEPT. One moment she was lying beside her mother, listening to the wind, and the next she was opening her eyes to stillness. Slipping out from under the covers, she padded to the window.

"Oh, is it morning?" her mother asked from the bed.

Hester pulled open the drapes and cracked the shutters. Moonlight picked out trees canted and toppled. "Not yet. I'm sorry for disturbing you."

She turned to find her mother sitting up in the bed. "At least that horrid storm is over. This is a very fine bed, but I prefer my own, and I'm sure you're eager to see Rebecca."

"I am," Hester admitted, coming back to her. "It must be close to dawn. Would you mind getting dressed now so we can leave as soon as the carriage is ready?"

Her mother agreed, and they lit a lamp and helped each other back into their gowns from the night before. The maid had draped them over a chest, so there were only a few wrinkles.

"Best we can do under such trying circumstances," her mother said with a sigh. "At least let me fix your hair."

Rob hadn't minded her hair down last night. She'd caught him eyeing it a time or two, as if he wondered how it would feel between his fingers. She sat down in front of the dressing table and wasn't surprised to find her cheeks turning pink.

A maid poked her head in just as Hester's mother finished putting in the last hairpin. The woman started at the sight of them. "You too?"

"Are the others up then?" Hester asked, rising from the dressing table.

"Miss Peverell, his lordship, the gentlemen," the maid said. "They're all in the green withdrawing room."

Hester and her mother found them there a short while later, all clustered around the window, which showed the pink bloom of dawn. Only Rob's sister was wearing something different than the night before.

"What's happened?" Hester's mother asked, venturing closer.

Rob immediately turned and shoved a spyglass at Mr. Donner, who fumbled to hold it against his waistcoat. "Nothing of any concern," he assured her with a smile that was far too bright. "I'll wager you're ready to head for home. I'll have the carriage brought around immediately."

Much as she longed to return to Rebecca, Hester could not shake the feeling he was rushing them.

"It looked to me that more than one tree was down," she allowed. "Can the carriage get through to Upper Grace?"

"No better time to find out," Rob said cheerily.

Elizabeth must have taken the spyglass from Mr. Donner, for she turned from the view with it in her hands. "There's no time, Rob. They'll be here too soon."

"Who?" Hester asked, even as Rob closed his eyes a moment as if saying a prayer.

Everyone looked to him. He nodded as if making a decision.

"A ship docked at our pier," he told her. "We don't know why."

Hester sucked in a breath. "Smugglers?"

"Right you are, missy," a voice behind them answered.

Hester turned with the others to find a heavy-set fellow standing in the doorway, cap pulled down over a fringe of iron-grey hair. His eyes were bloodshot, and stubble covered his bulbous chin. Far more menacing, however, was the pistol he held in one grip.

"Chalder?" Rob said, positioning himself in front of Hester. "What are you doing?"

"My job," he said. "My real job."

Mr. Donner darted forward. "You're a spy."

Hester edged around Rob in time to see Chalder draw himself up. "I am not. I'm a lander, like my father before me, and a good one. Neither of us was ever caught."

"I don't understand," Elizabeth put in. "What's a lander? Are you helping the smugglers?"

"I lead the smugglers," he informed her, head up with pride. "Leastwise, on land. It's my job to round up trustworthy types to carry the goods inland, away from the Preventers like our new Riding Surveyor. I call the tune as to when a ship may come in and how fast it's emptied."

"I suppose I'll find a blue spout lantern in my shed," Rob said, "suitable for signaling ships at sea."

"You'll find more than that if you look right now," Chalder told him. "I've a crew waiting to unload this ship and fill her with the information she'll carry back to France."

Donner stiffened.

"St. Claire or Ruggins?" Rob asked.

"Surely not Captain St. Claire," her mother protested.

Hester and Rosemary were among the few women who didn't favor the handsome formal naval officer. Still, she could not see him taking England's secrets to France.

Neither could Mr. Chalder, apparently, for he shook his head. "We have no business with the good captain, but that's all I'll say on the matter. Bad enough you had to see me."

"So what do you want from us, my good man?" Lord Featherstone put in. "I'm sure if it's a ransom you're after, our host can oblige."

"Always happy to support a worthy cause," Rob said, but the tone belied his words.

"We don't need your gold," the fellow spat out. "You wouldn't have even known we were here but for that storm. Now that the ship's come in, we'll commence unloading. Give us no trouble, and you can dine on the story for months. Decide to play the hero, and you'll be attending your own funeral instead." He cocked the pistol and leveled it at them. "Understand?"

Her mother, Elizabeth, Donner, and Lord Featherstone nodded. Rob merely eyed him as if he were a glob of mud spoiling the shine on his favorite pair of boots. Hester managed to catch his eye and shook her head just the slightest. The resolution in his gaze didn't waver.

"One of my men is holding most of your staff in the kitchen," Chalder warned. "Another has your coachman and his helpers in the stables, and a third is gathering up strays and then will come watch you lot. So long as you stay in this room, no harm will come to you. You'll know we've gone when you see the ship pulling away from the pier. Now, make yourselves comfortable."

No one moved.

He took another step into the room and pointed the gun at Rob. "Sit."

Elizabeth and Hester's mother hurried to perch on the sofa, and Mr. Donner and Lord Featherstone took up places on the chairs nearby. Still Rob stared the villain down, gaze mutinous. Her heart shouted a warning.

"Rob, please," she said as calmly as she could, taking a seat near her mother. "You promised me you'd changed."

He shuddered as if she'd struck him with a lash, but he flipped up his coattails and sank onto the chair by the hearth.

"Smart fellow," Chalder said. "Listen to your lady. You wouldn't want anything to happen to her."

Rob glared at him. "So much as touch her, and you're a dead man."

Chalder's gaze raked over her, cold as winter rain. Hester refused to gratify him with a shiver.

"Oh, you have nothing to fear from me, my lord," he said. "But I can't speak for the sailors on that ship. Rough types, they be. So, unless you want something to happen to any of these lovely ladies, you'll stay in your seat and learn patience."

Patience, the villain said. Rob's Achilles' heel. His wealth, status, and charm had meant he seldom had to wait. But he would do nothing now that might lead to Hester being harmed. He kept his mouth shut as Chalder backed from the room, then counted the seconds as the fellow's boots thumped down the stairs.

"Rob?" Elizabeth whispered, as if she had been listening too. "What shall we do?"

"Nothing," Mrs. Denby answered, glancing between him and Hester. "You heard the man. If we do not allow them to have their way, someone may be hurt."

The words stabbed him. Was this what it meant to be the viscount? To look the other way while evil triumphed because doing otherwise might be inconvenient? Yet, it wasn't just his inconvenience. He must think of Hester, Elizabeth, and the others.

"Mrs. Denby is correct," he made himself say. "Much as I would like to see these smugglers caught, we will remain in this room until we're certain they've gone."

Elizabeth's frown said she was disappointed in him. He

was disappointed in himself.

Donner went further. "You may have to wait, my lord," he said, pushing out of the chair, "but I made no such promise. This is what we've been expecting. I intend to act."

Elizabeth turned her frown on him. "William? What are you talking about?"

Rob shook his head at the intelligence agent, but Donner was apparently too caught up in the opportunity to pay him any regard.

"Forgive me, Miss Peverell," the intelligence agent said, snatching up the spyglass from where she had positioned it on the table next to the sofa. "I'm an intelligence agent for the War Office. I asked your brother to play along with the smugglers so we could capture their leader."

Now Hester was frowning, but at Rob. "Play along? You can't have been aiding these people."

"No," Rob assured her. "I offered Captain St. Claire the use of my pier, but no one's approached it until now."

"I find myself confused," Elizabeth said, in a tone that made Rob fight a shiver. "Was this the reason you found it necessary to visit the Lodge so frequently, Mr. Donner?"

Donner must not have noticed she'd stopped using his first name, for he positioned the spyglass at his eye as if he had far more important matters to attend to. "Of course."

"I knew it!" Elizabeth jumped to her feet and pointed a finger at Rob. "I knew he was up to something, and this proves it. I told you he was interesting."

Rob couldn't help his chuckle. "Yes, you did. I'm glad to hear that was the extent of your involvement with the fellow."

She glanced toward Donner, who remained oblivious. "I believe it was. A shame, actually. He isn't very good at his job if I could ferret him out that easily." She approached Donner and pried the spyglass from his fingers.

Donner stared at her. "What are you doing?"

"Returning this to someone who knows what he's about," Elizabeth told him. She brought the spyglass to Rob and handed it to him, then returned to her seat on the sofa, smile pleased.

Rob rose and went to join Donner by the window. The intelligence agent alternated between frowning and glancing at Elizabeth as reproachfully as a pup denied his favorite toy.

"I did advise you she would not take well to your attentions," Rob reminded him, raising the glass to his eye.

"Yes, well, you appear to have been right," Donner allowed. He squared his shoulders. "What do you see?"

Rob counted the men crossing his lawn. "Most of the sailors seem to have stayed at the pier or perhaps formed a chain up to the headland. Two wagons and their horses have appeared. I don't want to know how the inside of my shed looks if they've been holed up in it all night."

He felt Donner brush past as if to peer out the window himself. "Tubs—that's brandy. And those boxes are probably lace." His voice trembled with outrage.

Rob lowered the spyglass. "If that's the extent of their perfidy, Donner, be glad for it."

"It won't be." Donner turned from the view. "You heard Chalder. They intend to take information to France, likely information on England's defenses. We could lose the war from this very pier!"

Protests rang out around them.

"No!" Mrs. Denby cried.

"Not while I live," Lord Featherstone declared.

"Rob, you cannot allow it," Elizabeth insisted.

Rob looked to Hester. She was watching him. Waiting. Wanting him to be that steady, dependable fellow she, his sister, and his staff and his tenants needed, the fellow he'd worked so hard to become.

The person he would never be.

"Forgive me, Hester," he said. "I know what is expected of me, but I can't sit here and watch England's secrets go to France. If I can make the difference, I must act."

She rose and came around the sofa, and he steeled himself for her arguments, her pleas. She lay a hand on his arm and looked up into his eyes, her gaze determined.

"I understand, Rob. You have a responsibility not only to your family but to England."

One simple statement, and she wiped his slate clean. He drew in a breath, feeling as if it were the first he'd taken since his father had died. "Thank you. I promise you, whatever I do, I will protect you and the others."

She squeezed his arm. "I have the utmost faith in you. But, whatever you do, you will not be alone. I will be at your side."

CHAPTER EIGHTEEN

EARS TUNED FOR ANY MOVEMENT, Hester crept down the corridor with Rob and Mr. Donner. She'd had no time to question her decision. Even Rob hadn't argued overly much, as if he'd seen what this meant to her. They all knew time was of the essence. This fellow Chalder might claim he and the smugglers would leave after unloading their cargo, but what was to say they wouldn't take a hostage with them to prevent the rest from telling the authorities? She had to protect her mother, Elizabeth, and the others.

Especially Rob.

She glanced at him now. His eyes were narrowed, his face set in hard lines. Their goal was to escape the house and then determine what might be done. She slipped her hand into his and was rewarded with a smile.

They had just reached the landing when a gruff voice called, "Ho! Where do you think you're going?"

A tall, muscular fellow, black beard flecked with grey curling down to the middle of his chest, had come out of a room on the opposite wing, cutlass in one hand. Striped trousers flapping, he moved toward them, arm up and at the ready. She and the others froze.

Mr. Donner leaned closer to her and Rob. "I'll distract him. You run."

Rob nodded, but Hester eyed the space between the

smuggler and the stairs. "We won't make it."

Before anyone else could comment, a door opened in the wall near the smuggler, and Ike Bascom stepped out, fingers clutching a long-handled brass warming pan. Hester's heart sank. She shook her head at him, praying he would understand and save himself, but he strolled up to the smuggler and nodded politely.

"Morning, Mr. Sharpless. Having some trouble, are we?"

Hester stared at him, but she thought she heard Rob growl.

The smuggler frowned at Ike but returned the nod. "You're Henry Bascom's boy. Are you working for Mr. Chalder now?"

"No," Ike said, and he swung the warming pan hard. It clanged against the smuggler's grizzled head.

Hester took a step back as the fellow fell with a thud to the carpet at her feet.

"Sorry, my lord," Ike said to Rob as Mr. Donner hurried forward to relieve their fallen foe of his weapons. "After walking the corridors all night, I overslept, only to find this lot about. Where's everyone else?"

Hester managed a breath as Rob moved to clap the youth on his shoulder.

"Most of the staff is in the kitchen," he explained, "being watched by another of these ruffians. Can you and Mr. Donner secure this fellow and then free them?"

Mr. Donner glanced up from where he'd crouched beside the smuggler. "What do you intend to do, my lord?"

To Hester's surprise, he looked to her. "What do you think of our chances of reaching the village and bringing back help?"

She gathered her thoughts with difficulty. "I've heard there's a path behind St. Andrew's that leads up onto the Lodge headland. If we can find it through the debris from the storm, we'll come out at the church."

"And the magistrate's home is right next door," Rob said with a grin. "Sounds like an adventure to me."

It did to her too, but immediately she saw the problem. How could they make the journey and return in time to catch the smugglers? Mind sorting through options, she turned to Mr. Donner, who had risen to stand beside Ike, cutlass in his hand, while the smuggler lay at his feet.

"You mentioned a distraction, Mr. Donner," she said. "What we need is a delay."

Ike nodded. "A good lander will have that ship cleared in less than an hour."

"Only if he has a good crew," Hester reasoned. "A crew that has, apparently, been hiding in a shed for most of the night."

"They'll want food, water," Rob pointed out.

Hester's conviction grew. "If we lace it with something to make them drowsy, that might slow their progress enough so we can return with aid."

"Our physician in London prescribed laudanum for Elizabeth," Rob offered. "Her maid, Kinsey, will know where to find it."

"But how can we get them to eat it?" Donner protested. "They aren't likely to trust us."

"They'll trust me," Ike predicted. "That's at least something to be said for being the son of a smuggler."

"It's decided then," Rob said. "Good luck, gentlemen. Hester, I will follow your lead."

Hester smiled. The smugglers of Grace-by-the-Sea had just met their match.

Her optimism carried her out the front door. The sight that met her eyes brought her up short.

Two of the trees had fallen across the drive, their trunks splintered by the crash, limbs twisted like fingers reaching for the sky. Branches broken from other trees and bushes lay here, there, everywhere. A fitful wind plucked at them and set them to rocking as if they sought to flee as well. The tang of the sea hung in the air. Everything shouted at her to turn back.

She squared her shoulders. "This way."

As if he had complete faith in her, Rob followed.

It took her a little while to thread her way through the debris, every moment like a ticking clock in her head, but she managed to locate the path to the village, and they started down. Below, she could see over most of the rooftops of Grace-by-the-Sea. More than one was missing shingles. Even the thatched cottages looked battered, odd pieces sticking up, like brooding hens with ruffled feathers.

They reached the bottom of the path near St. Andrew's, and Rob gave her hand a tug. Together, they ran around the churchyard to the house next to it and through its front garden to pound at the door. Hester's heart leaped when the magistrate's mother, Mrs. Howland, answered.

"Hester, Lord Peverell?" she said, blinking. "Have you come from the Lodge? Is everything all right?"

"No," Hester said, stumbling into the warm front hall. "We need help."

"Smugglers have overtaken the Lodge," Rob explained. "We've come to alert the magistrate."

Mrs. Howland gripped Hester's arm as if she would keep her in place from sheer force of will. "He's not here. He, the vicar, your brother, and all the men of the militia are out rescuing families from the aftermath of that storm. Trees came down on houses and shops. Two oaks fell to block the entrances to the castle. We wouldn't have known if Miranda hadn't shinnied through the wreckage and run to the village to tell us."

Rob sagged. "Then we'll never stop the smugglers in time."

Hester raised her head. "Yes, we will. The magistrate and the Men's Militia aren't the only valiant fighters in this area. Grace-by-the-Sea has a Women's Militia, and I know who leads it. We must find Abigail Bennett."

Rob had left the Lodge with Hester at his side, but he returned with a veritable army at his back. Hester had located Abigail Bennett in the center of the village, directing the work of repairing some of the shops that had had windows blown in.

"We'll call out the Women's Militia," the painter promised after Hester had told her what had happened at the Lodge. "Some are securing their homes, but I'm sure we can find enough to rout these brigands. Still, we might want to ensure we have something to fall back on in case they reach the ship and set sail." She nodded to a woman who had been helping her. "Maisy—find Captain St. Claire and tell him we have need of the *Siren's Call* off the west headland."

In the end, Abigail; Mrs. Catchpole, the employment agency owner; the Misses Pierce of the linens and trimmings shop; Mrs. Ellison, the wife of the baker; Mrs. Mance, Hester's assistant teacher; three other ladies of the village; Jesslyn Denby; and Mrs. Tully followed them up the headland. The women were armed with staves for the most part, though Abigail had a sword at her hip. Hester had explained that Jesslyn's father, Dr. Chance, had taught Abigail to handle a sword when she was a girl, in part so she could protect herself from an abusive father.

And the irony was not lost on him that he was being saved by a group of women, led by the one lady he'd left behind but never forgotten.

She marched beside him as they threaded their way up the headland. The sea breeze tugged free a strand of her honey-colored hair. Rob reached out to tuck it behind her ear. She blushed.

"Keep low and behind trees as much as you can when we come out at the top," Abigail advised from ahead of them. Tall, slender, and dressed in a long coat and breeches, he might have mistaken her for a lad except for that cap of red hair styled in a bun at the back of her neck.

Hester passed Abigail's advice back down the column.

"We should have waited for the trolls," Mrs. Tully lamented.

The trees were bare enough, the bushes torn by the storm, that it wasn't easy to sneak up on the Lodge. Still, all activity appeared to be at the back, for they managed to reach the northeast corner near the kitchen addition without seeing anyone.

The storm, however, had left its mark on his property. More than one tree was down or canted to one side, branches hanging. As he, Abigail, and Hester peered around the corner into the rear yard, he spotted more branches spread across the grass, slowing the movements of those who were working to unload the ship.

Much as he decried the practice, he had to admire their ingenuity. As each item of contraband reached the headland, men stood ready to accept it. Chalder stood in the middle of it all, directing a man here, ordering another there. Some carried the crates and boxes to waiting wagons, where they were secreted in false bottoms or tucked behind duty-paid goods. Others strapped tubs front and back, like ungainly mules, and took off at a trot out around the crooked wing. Those items must be for closer deliveries, and he could only wonder who else in the area was profiting from the work of the Lord of the Smugglers.

"We should check the kitchen," Hester whispered. "See what happened."

Rob motioned the ladies to keep down, then edged back to the kitchen door and eased himself higher to peer through the window in it. Bascom, Monsieur Antoine, Eckman, Kinsey, and a number of maids were clustered around the worktable in the center, Elizabeth, Lord Featherstone, and Mrs. Denby with them. He opened the door and stepped inside.

They all tensed, then beamed as he came into the room, Hester, Abigail, and the Women's Militia right behind.

"Well met, my lord," Lord Featherstone said, coming to clasp his hand. He and Elizabeth had armed themselves with swords. They looked suspiciously like the ones that had hung on the wall in the formal withdrawing room. And he could not quite accustom himself to seeing Mrs. Denby clutching a mace.

She hurried to hug her daughter now, careful to keep the spiked ball away from her.

"What's the news?" Rob asked. "Were you able to hand them poison food?"

"Poison!" From the way the chef yelped the word, Rob might have thought he'd suggested that the fellow serve himself on a platter. "My food is not bad."

Bascom pushed forward. "He means the laudanum, sir. And yes, they were eager to lap up whatever we could give them. But we haven't noticed it slowing them down just yet."

"It's almost as if they were taking their time, waiting," Elizabeth agreed.

"For the information they want to take back to France," Rob realized. Then he frowned, glancing around. "Where is Donner?"

Elizabeth wrinkled her nose. "Outside somewhere. Spying."

"I believe he called it evaluation," Lord Featherstone put in diplomatically.

"Then we have one more ally," Abigail said. "What do you advise, my lord?"

Rob looked back at her, and a shadow crossed the window, a smuggler, shoving another man in front of him.

Rob groaned. "Stand ready. I need to rescue someone."

He darted out the door before any of them could stop him.

The smuggler had just reached the corner of the house. Rob threw himself at the fellow, knocking him off his feet and plummeting after him.

Mercer clutched his portfolio to his scrawny chest, staring down at them. "See here! What is the meaning of this?"

"Run!" Rob ordered, wrestling with the smuggler. "You're in danger."

Pounding footsteps proved as much. Both Chalder and another smuggler were on him a moment later. The smuggler hauled him to his feet. The fellow he'd knocked down surged up and smashed a fist into his gut. Rob struggled not to double as pain lanced him. In the distance, he thought he heard a cry, as if someone else had felt the blow as well.

"Enough!" Mercer shrieked, scurrying up to Chalder. "You promised no one would be hurt."

Rob stared at him, unwilling to accept what he was hearing.

"He doesn't know when to do as he's told," the lander grumbled.

Mercer snorted. "That much is true. I thought I had matters well in hand, but this trip to London, my contacts informed me that he and that Donner fellow are working for the War Office. Which is why I'll be sailing with my information this time."

CHAPTER NINETEEN

AS CHALDER ORDERED THE OTHER two smug-glers back to work, Rob rounded on his steward. "You're the one passing information to the French?"

"That should be apparent." Mercer shook his head, still treating Rob as if he were an unruly youth and the steward an Eton don. "You, of course, were not supposed to know about any of it. That will be a problem."

"Your problem, not mine," Chalder said. "I've enough to worry about now that he's seen me and several of my men. We'll have to relocate, and that won't be easy."

"I must relocate as well," Mercer informed him. "I have already cleared out my apartments in London. I have been staying in the village the last few days, waiting for the ship. I saw it coming in this morning and managed to pick my way up the headland. Now, I shall be leaving England for a nice chateau on Lake Geneva."

Chalder crossed his arms over his chest and widened his stance. "Some of my men won't like you turning tail."

Mercer smirked. "You can do nothing to me. I am used to dealing with endless amounts of paper. Did you think I would leave nothing behind if something should happen to me?"

Chalder dropped his arms. "You," he said to Rob, "I want you where I can see you." He jerked his head around the corner of the house, and Rob started walking.

Mercer accompanied him. "Don't do anything rash, my lord. Think of your sister. You would not want to give her another family member to grieve."

Rob could have overpowered him in a moment, but one shout would bring the smugglers down on him anew, and he could not chance that they might check the kitchen and find everyone else before the women and the others were ready.

"Let me go, Mercer," he murmured, "and I promise I will plead for leniency."

Mercer shook his head again. "We are far beyond leniency, my lord. But you won't say a word against me, whatever happens. A shame you didn't sign that lease for Captain Ruggins yesterday. That would have made all this far messier for you to bring to court. But I haven't forgotten how many times your father had to pay a gambling debt or offer coin to keep someone from pressing charges with the magistrate after some ill-chosen actions following a night of drinking. That's all in writing too, carefully saved. I could ruin you with a single article in the *Times*."

"You've thought of everything, it seems," Rob said as they reached the rear yard. Both wagons had gone, and the stream of goods up from the pier had become a trickle.

But Hester's plan was working. A smuggler stumbled here, yawned there. Another sank down onto the grass and did not rise.

Beside him, Mercer preened. "A shame you finally appreciate my talents. I have a skill for enriching myself, one way or another."

"Including selling England's secrets to France," Rob accused, stopping near the stables.

"They pay well," Mercer said, as if they were discussing a counting house and not England's greatest enemy. "And it's not as if the French can ever beat our defenses. Why shouldn't I make a little profit at their expense?"

"Why indeed," Rob agreed. He edged toward the stable door. If he could just free Mr. Fitch and his men, Hester and Abigail might have enough numbers to overwhelm the smugglers.

Mercer tsked. "I wouldn't do that if I were you. Mr. Chalder is concerned enough for his future that it wouldn't take much to convince him you must go. I've already looked into your hereditary line. You are the last male Peverell. Should anything happen to you, your sister will keep the London house, but the estate in Wiltshire will default to the Crown with the title. Perhaps if she sells the hunting box in Scotland and this monstrosity, she might be able to eke out an existence."

He painted a bleak picture. All Rob had done to change, all the duty he owed his sister, tenants, and staff, all could be undone if he made the wrong choice now.

Chalder stalked back to their sides. "It's all arranged. You'll be sailing with the tide, Mr. Mercer."

Mercer smiled. "Thank you, Mr. Chalder. Good day, my lord." He minced off toward the path down to the pier.

"You're aiding France in the war," Rob accused the lander. "How can you live with that on your conscience?"

Chalder hitched up his breeches. "I sleep well enough at night." He glanced out at his men and frowned. "What's wrong with you lot? Someone may come looking to see how the Peverells weathered the storm. Move!"

Smugglers stumbled and bumped into each other. Two more fell to the trampled grass.

Chalder rounded on Rob. "What have you done?"

"Me?" Rob asked. "I'm merely enjoying the farce."

"Well, we'll see if you enjoy it so much when I send you to France with Mr. Mercer."

Hester paced the kitchen, until Bascom turned from the window to face the waiting group. "They've taken him around the back of the house," he reported.

"What will they do with him?" Elizabeth asked, voice trembling.

"More's to the point, what should we do that won't endanger him?" Abigail asked.

Hester glanced around at them all, from the Women's Militia with their staves cut from broomsticks to her mother clutching a spiked iron ball. They were so determined, so ready to act.

And every one of them looked to her for leadership.

"We will rescue Lord Peverell," she vowed.

Elizabeth and Abigail nodded, but Hester could only blink as her vehement words echoed in the room. Where had they come from? Who was she to say what might happen? Everything in her life had been happenstance.

Even Rob's return to her life.

Yet, Rob didn't expect her to be helpless. He had been quite willing to have her call the tune, to follow where she'd led. He clearly saw something she hadn't realized she possessed.

Fortitude.

Everything that had happened to her, everything she'd learned, had built into a solid strength inside her. She wasn't helpless. She could do this, for herself and for the man she loved.

Abigail, Elizabeth, and the others were waiting expectantly. Hester drew in a breath.

"How close are they to leaving, Ike?" she asked.

"They're about done unloading, as far as I can tell," he replied. "It shouldn't be long now, but I wouldn't want to wait. I'm not sure what they plan to do to his lordship."

That was her fear as well. "And what about the two smugglers we captured?" she asked. "Won't someone come looking for them?"

"Taken care of," one of the maids said. "We dosed them with laudanum too, and Mr. Eckman managed to slip them down closer to the pier."

Another maid swished her skirts back and forth. "And I put a bottle of wine in each hand. With any luck, the others will think they were overcome and bring them aboard to sleep it off, no one the wiser."

"Well done," Hester said, and the maid beamed. "The others should become groggy too, thanks to Monsieur Antoine."

The chef inclined his head. "They will never know what happened. You are an exceptional woman to recognize that I have the blood of warriors in my veins. This is my finest hour!"

"The men on the ship are another story," Abigail predicted. "They'll be eager to sail before a revenue cutter shows up. We can only hope Maisy found Captain St. Claire, and the *Siren's Call* is on its way."

At the mention of the captain, many of the women exchanged glances, grinning.

"Make yourselves ready, then," Hester said. "We'll go through the dining room and out the doors there. That should put us in the middle of them, where Abigail and the Women's Militia can attack more easily. I will find Lord Peverell."

As her mother turned to point the Women's Militia in the right direction, Elizabeth gave Hester a quick hug.

"You better marry my brother," she ordered. "I already consider you a sister."

On the way out the kitchen door for the house, her mother gave Hester a look as if to say *I told you so.*

Marry Rob. Well, that was a choice Hester would have to make, if it were offered.

"Think, Chalder," Rob urged as the lander shoved him toward the path to the ship. "If your captain kidnaps a peer of the realm, none of you will ever escape. You'll be hunted down and hung."

"I'll take my chances," the smuggler said. "The others may have seen me, but it's your word that would have me convicted. If you're not around to tell anyone, all the better for me."

Rob was wracking his brain for a way to escape when the glass-paned doors of the dining room burst open, and Hester rushed out into the yard.

Rob's heart leaped to his throat, and he jerked away from the lander. The other smugglers rallied, heading toward her. He'd never reach her before they surrounded her.

He didn't have to. Behind her streamed the members of the Women's Militia, staves up and voices raised in challenge. With them came Bascom, armed with a rolling pin; Lord Featherstone and Elizabeth with their swords; and Eckman and Monsieur Antoine with cleavers in their grips. As if emboldened by the sight of them, his coachman and grooms came pouring out of the stables to join them, and Donner popped out of a bush at a run.

The remaining smugglers took one look at them all and fled.

Chalder grabbed Rob by the scruff of the neck with one hand, pistol in the other, and stood his ground. "Go back to the house," he told Hester's army, "or his lordship dies."

"Leave him alone!" Hester ordered, and his staff converged on the lander. Around them, he spotted others chasing the smugglers down the hill.

Chalder aimed the pistol at Bascom, switched to Eckman, then dropped the gun entirely as Monsieur Antoine, face florid and mustache flourishing, raised his clever at the fellow. Eckman grabbed the lander and marched him off to be secured in the stables until the magistrate could be called.

Hester threw herself into Rob's arms. "Are you all right?"

With her held close, the world seemed right at last. "Never better." He leaned back to smile at her. "Did you and your friends just subdue a vicious smuggling ring that has evaded even the authorities?"

She glanced around to where the women were rounding up the smugglers on the lawn. "I suppose we did. Who would have guessed?"

"I would," Rob assured her. "You are one of the most capable women I know, Hester. You give children knowledge for a better future. You help your family, your friends. You point me in the right direction, guide me on the best path."

Her sweet lips trembled. "If I have done all that, I am glad."

He tucked her close once more, relishing the feel of her against him. "So, when this is over, what shall we do next? Ride for Weymouth and berate the Excise Office for its shocking lack of foresight to allow smugglers to roam unimpeded?"

Hester shook her head, hair tickling his chin. "You forget, sir. My brother is employed by the Excise Office. I assure you he works tirelessly to stop smugglers."

"Then, in deference to your brother, I will do no more than write a scathing letter to the king about the matter," Rob told her. "That's what viscounts do, apparently. Write letters. Sign papers."

She must have heard the frustration in his voice, for she leaned back and stroked a hair from his forehead, the touch warm. "You would not find Weymouth all that interesting in any regard. Far too proper. Even the king bathes there on occasion."

He chuckled. "I've always wanted to see the king bathing."

"That I doubt," Hester said, but she joined his laugh. "And if bathing interests you so much, I'm sure Jesslyn would be delighted to include you when next they take the bathing huts out into the cove. I understand it's very bracing."

Rob kept his gaze on Hester. "I'm game if you are. I imagine you look rather fetching in a bathing smock."

She blushed. "Ladies and gentlemen bathe separately, sir. The position of the huts prevents them from seeing each other."

"I'm sure I could convince someone to reposition the huts," he mused.

"You should not," Hester scolded.

"You see?" he challenged. "Keeping me proper, just as I said."

"Well," Hester countered, "someone should."

He braced his hands on her hips. "And I wish that someone would always be you. I love you, Hester."

She sucked in a breath, eyes widening. "What did you say?"

He raised his voice, determined that everyone should hear a declaration that had been too long in coming. "I said I love you. You would make the perfect viscountess. Will you marry me?"

Passing with a smuggler in hand, Bascom grinned. The women closest to them dropped their weapons to applaud. Mrs. Tully gave him two thumbs up.

His beautiful love merely stared at him.

"Hester?" Rob swallowed, throat suddenly tight. "Am I wrong about your feelings? Do you care nothing for me after all?"

More of her army wandered closer. Her mother nudged Hester's shoulder. "Answer him, Hester. He's asking you to marry him."

"I believe he is considered quite the catch," Lord Feath-erstone put in kindly.

"You could well be the making of him, Mrs. Todd," Donner agreed.

"Tell him yes," Elizabeth begged.

Hester straightened away from him, and a hush fell. Rob felt it to his toes. He was too late. He wasn't the man she wanted after all. She was going to refuse him.

CHAPTER TWENTY

THEY WERE ALL WATCHING HER, ready to offer suggestions. Hester didn't need anyone's advice. She didn't need anyone's permission. She knew what she wanted. Once, she and Rob had been all about the excitement of illicit romance. Now their feelings were based on something stronger, more enduring: friendship, trust. Love. This was her choice.

"I care for you far more than is wise," she told Rob. "And I hate imagining the future without you in it. So, yes, Rob, I will marry you."

Huzzahs rang out around them. Rob pulled her back into his arms. One kiss, to seal their future. One kiss, to promise her love.

One kiss that confirmed she had made the right choice.

"Thank you," he said as he disengaged. "You cannot know how happy you've made me. I promise to do all I can to see that you don't regret this decision."

"Oh, Rob," she said. "How could I regret marrying the only man I've ever truly loved?"

His eyes lit, and he was kissing her again. As if from a long distance, she heard a cough.

Rob pulled back and frowned at Ike. "This had better be important, Bascom."

The young footman nodded solemnly. "It is, my lord. I thought you and Mrs. Todd would want to see."

Rob slipped his arm about her waist, and they both turned to find everyone gazing out at the Channel. It seemed the women who had followed the smugglers to the ship had lost their skirmish, for the vessel was veering out into the Channel, borne on the tide and wind.

"No!" Hester cried, stiffening. "They shouldn't be getting away. Where are Captain St. Claire and his men?"

Abigail sheathed her sword to stride back to their sides. "Maybe Maisy couldn't find him. I would have liked to have stopped the entire smuggling band, but perhaps it's enough those sailors know they are not welcome in Grace-by-the-Sea."

"I heartily agree," Rob said. "The Women's Militia has done the village a service." He glanced around at those gathered near. "You all have done the village, and me, a service. I will not forget it."

From those closest to the cliffs, a shout went up. Rob inclined his head, as if he thought it commendation, but Hester saw what excited them. Another ship, black sides sleek, was cutting through the water, giving chase to the smugglers.

"It's the *Siren's Call*," Ike declared. "The captain's after them!"

More huzzahs echoed as Captain St. Claire's ship gained ground on the smugglers' vessel. Something boomed, loud enough to be heard on the shore, and water fountained next to the criminals' ship. When the second boom came, Hester spotted the flash of gunpowder.

The smugglers' ship canted, and the *Siren's Call* swooped closer. Slowly, as if reluctantly, the other vessel turned toward shore to anchor off the headland.

Rob looked to Hester. "I imagine St. Claire will be rowed ashore shortly. I'd like to hear what he has to say."

"So would I," Hester assured him.

In the end, all the members of the Women's Militia, Rob's staff, and Lord Featherstone and Donner were waiting when Quillan St. Claire and Alexander Chance strode into the yard. Alex had his pistol trained on a small, slender man, who stumbled along, clutching his portfolio to his chest.

Rob started grinning.

"Who is that?" Hester asked as they approached.

"That," Rob said, "is my steward and a traitor to England if there ever was one. Nice job, Chance."

"Tell that to Hester," Alex said. "We wouldn't have known to set sail if she and Abigail hadn't sent Maisy to us."

Mercer managed to wrest himself away from Hester's brother-in-law. "This is the outside of enough. I am an English citizen."

"An English citizen bound for Switzerland after carrying tales to France," Rob amended. "I'm sure the War Office would like a few words."

Donner stepped forward. "We would indeed, particularly as to how it became known that Lord Peverell and I were working to capture the Lord of the Smugglers."

"Were you?" Captain St. Claire drawled. "Well, we are happy to oblige, aren't we, Chance?"

"Of course," Alex agreed.

Aunt Maudie, who had been standing nearby, leaned closer to Hester. "Did you see that?" His ears twitched. That means he's lying."

Lying? Why would Alex not be happy to capture the Lord of the Smugglers?

The steward struggled in his grip. "You'll pay for this outrage, Captain St. Claire," he vowed. "Your name's already on Napoleon's list of enemies. After today, you're a dead man."

St. Claire shrugged. "I've been considered one too many times to count. If Napoleon wants me, he'll have to fetch me himself." He nodded to Ike. "Mr. Bascom. Would you be willing to lend a hand?"

"It would be my privilege," Ike assured him before joining Alex in hustling Mercer around the house. As if determined to watch, Aunt Maudie trotted after them.

"Where will you take them?" Hester asked as more smugglers were escorted past by the members of the Women's Militia and the Peverell staff.

"To Castle How for the time being so your brother can question them," St. Claire replied. "The castle cellar is large enough to hold them, and it has a stout lock. We won't lack for guards after this. You're well regarded among the locals, my lord. I doubt they'll take kindly to you being inconvenienced."

Rob pulled her closer. "It was an adventure, one my betrothed and I hope not to repeat."

Captain St. Claire glanced between them. "Ah, love. A curious affliction."

Hester smiled. "One I hope someday afflicts you as well, Captain."

He inclined his head. "I'm afraid that ship may have sailed, Mrs. Todd, but time will tell."

Rob led Hester and his remaining guests inside. "As soon as Mr. Fitch is ready, I'll have him take you back to the village," he promised Lord Featherstone and Donner.

Donner gave him a tight smile. "I have work at the castle. I think I'll walk. Care to join me, my lord?"

"Delighted," Lord Featherstone said. "But I should return my weaponry first."

"Allow me," Mrs. Denby said, juggling her mace so she could accept the baron's sword as well. "I'll need to stay. Someone must help Miss Peverell chaperone her brother and his bride."

She and Elizabeth exchanged pleased smiles.

"Thank you, my lord," Rob said, trying to ignore his irrepressible sister. He and Hester saw Donner and Lord Featherstone off, then Rob led Hester, her mother, and Elizabeth to the formal withdrawing room, where Mrs. Denby returned the sword to its hanger on the wall and the mace to the grip of a suit of armor. Elizabeth hung up her sword as well.

"Those haven't been sharpened in years, you know," Rob felt compelled to point out.

His sister winked at him. "A good thing the smugglers didn't know that." She made a show of settling herself on one of the chairs near the hearth. Mrs. Denby went to join her.

Rob sat instead on the sofa, with Hester beside him.

She sighed. "I can't believe it's over and we won."

"Because of you," Rob assured her, taking her hand.

"And now?" she asked.

He eyed her. "Now we marry. I distinctly heard you promise as much."

"I did," she agreed. "But should we wait until you finish mourning?"

He glanced toward Elizabeth. His sister must have been watching them, listening, for she answered Hester's question with a vehement shake of her head.

"No," Rob said, facing Hester anew. "My father and mother would understand. There is a matter of securing the line. And things are less fussy in the country than in London. I doubt any here will fault us, especially when we are merely following the earl's good example."

"Very well," she said. "I'm not sure I'd want to wait so long in any regard. I love you, Rob."

He claimed her lips. One kiss, to seal his promise. One kiss, to show her how much he valued her.

One kiss that confirmed she was the perfect bride for him.

"Then let's get married today," he said as she withdrew.

She started laughing even as he heard a squeak of protest from her mother.

"No, Rob," Hester said. "It would require a special license, which can only be had in London, at least a twelve-hour ride away. And Elizabeth needs you here. You will simply have to wait until the banns to be called."

"The banns?" He collapsed against the back of the sofa. "That takes three weeks! I won't survive."

Hester bent and kissed him again. "I promise you will. I love you too much, Rob."

And that was all that mattered, in the end. She loved him, with all his foibles and follies. If he had wondered whether he had a purpose in this world, he had found it in her.

One Week Later

ROB DREW IN A DEEP breath of the brine-scented air and tucked Hester's arm more securely in his as they watched Rebecca attempt to convince Bascom to try the kite once more on the narrow rear lawn of the Lodge. Rob had offered the young footman a permanent position on his staff, pleasing them both. Monsieur Antoine had been so moved by the encounter that he had vowed fidelity as well.

"I am proud to see my masterpieces served to a lady and gentleman who would stare down the tyrant's brigands," he'd declared when he'd personally brought Rob dinner the first night after the smugglers had been caught.

Just as they had the summer they'd met, Hester had spent part of every day with Rob since. Rebecca was generally with them, though her grandmother watched her on occasion. Mrs. Denby had been delighted to tell anyone who'd listen that her daughter was going to marry Lord Peverell.

The only fly in the ointment had been the disposition of the dame school in Upper Grace.

"Apparently viscountesses don't teach," Hester had said with a sigh when she'd been notified by the church leaders they intended to seek a new teacher.

Rob had put his arm about her. "My viscountess can do what she likes. If they won't have you, talk to Mr. Wingate. Grace-by-the-Sea has needed its own school for some time. I'm sure a thousand pounds would cover it."

Hester had laughed.

Rebecca brought the kite back to him now, holding it up, lips tight. "The tail is too short."

Rob crouched beside her to examine the bits of paper, stick, and rag. "Is it now? How long should a good tail be, do you think?"

"As long as my arm," Rebecca informed him, stretching out her hand. "You must learn such things. You're going to be my father."

Rob smiled at her. "Yes, I am."

She wiggled. "I knew it before anyone else."

Hester turned away to hide a smile.

"Yes, you did," Rob agreed. "You're a very clever young lady."

"I'm your daughter," she said, and she gave him a hug that included the kite.

Throat tight, he held her a moment, gaze meeting Hester's to find it warm and tearing.

"Would you like to play with the kite?" Rebecca asked as she disengaged. "After we fix the tail, of course."

"Delighted," Rob said, rising and picking her and the kite up as well. "Let's see what your aunt Elizabeth can contrive. She's very good at this sort of thing."

"Swords too," Rebecca said, at which Hester's brows went up.

"I won't allow her to play with anything sharp," Rob promised her as they headed for the Lodge.

"You can try," Hester warned.

How good she was for him. He would never be the staid, unexceptional viscount he had tried to be. Likely, his father, mother, and brother would have expected it, but he could only be his own person, do his duty his own way. There was a joy in leading, protecting, and encouraging. Hester would help him remember that.

If he had had any doubts whether she would be comfortable at his side, she'd swiftly put them to rest in the last week. She'd located Mr. Priestly, who worked as secretary to the magistrate. The orderly running of the village meant that the man had time on his hands, so he had agreed to act as Rob's agent in Dorset as well. Already, he'd set matters to rights where Mercer had changed them for his own profit.

Donner had brought the former steward personally to the War Office. If they didn't charge him for treason, he would be prosecuted for embezzlement and endangerment. They would not be seeing the fellow again.

They might not see much of Donner either. Now that everyone knew he was an intelligence agent, and not a tremendously good one, he would be reassigned elsewhere. If the War Office chose to send someone else their way, Rob could only hope the fellow would be more circumspect, and less necessary.

"Two more weeks," he reminded Hester as Rebecca and Elizabeth worked on the kite in his mother's withdrawing room. Spending time with the little girl was helping chase away the last of Elizabeth's doldrums, and he was glad to see his sister smile far more often.

"Does it truly trouble you to wait to hear the banns read?" Hester asked beside him.

Rob brought her hand to his lips for a kiss. "No. I like hearing my name linked with yours. And you are worth the wait, then and now."

"And you were the suitor worth a second chance," she assured him. "I'll always be thankful you returned to Grace-by-the-Sea and to me."

"So will I," he told her. "Being the viscount means I must spend some time each year in London to attend Parliament. But I promise you, we will return here, again and again, because this is where you made a man of me."

"This is where we both remembered our dreams," she said. "To stand beside each other. Forever."

DEAR READER
      Thank you for choosing Hester and Rob's story. I've always had a soft spot for first loves reuniting. If you do too, and you haven't read the other books in the series, you might try the first book, *The Matchmaker's Rogue*, to see how Jesslyn and her love Lark, Hester's brother, came back to each other.

If you enjoyed this book, there are several things you could do now:

Sign up for a free email newsletter at https://subscribe. reginascott.com so you'll be the first to know when a new book is out or on sale. I offer exclusive, free short stories to my subscribers from time to time. Don't miss out.

Connect with me on Facebook at http://www.face-book.com/authorreginascott, BookBub at https://www.bookbub.com/authors/regina-scott, or Pinterest at http://www.pinterest.com/reginascottpins.

Post a review on a bookseller site, BookBub, or Goodreads to help others find the book.

Discover my many other books on my website at www.reginascott.com.

Turn the page for a peek at the sixth book in the Grace-by-the-Sea series, *The Siren's Captain*. Privateer Quillan St. Claire fears no man, not even Napoleon, who is breathing out threats against him for the many times Quill has thwarted his plans to invade England. But when a French soprano arrives in Grace-by-the-Sea with a message from the tyrant, the valiant captain may truly be in danger at last, of losing his heart.

Blessings!

Regina Scott

SNEAK PEEK:

REGINA SCOTT

CHAPTER ONE

Grace-by-the-Sea, Dorset, England, October 1804

QUILLAN ST. CLAIRE, FORMERLY OF His Majesty's Navy, leaned against the pale blue walls of the assembly rooms and scanned the well-dressed attendees at the annual Autumn Serenade. Row upon row of chairs crossed the polished wood floor, all aimed at a dais that had been erected under the musicians' alcove at the head of the room. He applauded politely as Mrs. Marjorie Howland, mother of his friend James, finished a sweet melody on her harp. That was the eighth act of local talent since he'd walked in the door, and at least a few had gone before he'd arrived fashionably late.

Arriving at all had been his first mistake. He enjoyed good music as much as the next fellow, and it was nice to see his neighbors show off skills they generally reserved for family. But he had no family here. He was the outsider, the stranger. Oh, he had no doubt the people of Grace-by-the-Sea would welcome him into their homes. He'd been invited enough times when he made his rare appearances at church services, the assemblies, or the spa that formed the backbone of the local economy.

It was better to remain aloof. Safer for his work. And he certainly didn't want anyone guessing who was behind the rumors of a Lord of the Smugglers plying his trade hereabouts.

He almost left then, but he gave the room one last scan.

His appearance would be worth the effort if he located the latest French agent to infiltrate the little village. They had been arriving with alarming regularity since Napoleon had begun massing his troops across the Channel with the intention of invading England: French spies masquerading as spa visitors, smuggling rings intent on taking England's secrets to France. He knew the smuggling trade. He had enough friends among the Royalists hiding in France that he could bring back information England badly needed to stop the tyrant.

So long as no one suspected that was his true motive for sailing out at night.

But everywhere he looked, he saw faces he'd been seeing since he'd come to live in Dove Cottage at the top of the village three years ago. He could rule out anyone associated with the vaunted Spa Corporation Council. The members and their families were located near the front, right behind the row of Regulars, those visitors who could not seem to pry themselves from the elegant spa. He recognized the silver-haired mane of Lord Featherstone and the auburn tresses of Mrs. Harding, who had recently returned to their shores with her betrothed, Mr. Warfield Crabapple.

Nearby were the ranking members of the area—Lord Peverell, his sister, and his betrothed, the widow Mrs. Todd, as well as the dowager Countess of Howland, her recently wed son, and his bride. Only the last gave him any twinge of concern, and not because he suspected her of spying. The former Rosemary Denby had once made it apparent she would have liked him to pursue her acquaintance. He'd rebuffed her, soundly. A mistake that. There weren't many ladies with her intellect, wit, and courage.

Not that he was looking to further his acquaintance with any lady. Though he had been interested any number of times, the all-consuming love that had claimed so many of the eligible bachelors of Grace-by-the-Sea had never overtaken him. He began to think himself immune. Sadly.

He kept his gaze moving over the merchants near the back, the servants standing along the walls, waiting to be of assistance to their mistresses and masters, the Inchley family, who managed the rooms. No one looked particularly out of place.

He puffed out a sigh. He prided himself on being a particularly keen observer. He had subscribed to Lord Nelson's approach before he'd even heard of Britain's Naval leader. Knowing what a person wanted and supplying it or threatening to deny it had seen him through his earliest years at the foundling home in London, his short tenure at Eton, and his rise through the ranks of the navy.

His skills had failed when it came to the French spies that continued to sneak into the area. Indeed, the villains had been largely uncovered through the agency of the ladies of Grace-by-the-Sea, who had proven themselves a savvy lot.

Dignified in his evening black, James stepped up onto the dais then, as he had for all the previous performers. "Thank you, Mother."

As the lady moved off the dais and Mr. Inchley came to position her harp to one side, James faced the audience. He might never have served on the deck of a frigate, but that short-cropped blond hair, features that ought to have been carved in stone, and muscular build lent him an air of command.

"We are fortunate to have such a generous group of friends and neighbors willing to share their talents with us," he told the audience. "Another round of applause, if you please."

The soft thud of gloved hands clapping filled the room with quiet thunder.

"And another, if I may," he continued, "for Lord Peverell, who graciously funded the event."

More applause. Peverell inclined his tawny head in acknowledgment while his sister, bride-to-be, and her mother beamed at him.

"And now," James said, magistrate's voice echoing in the room, "I have the pleasure of introducing you to our most prestigious performer, Mademoiselle Marie-Louise Fortier, fresh from her triumph at Drury Lane in London and her performance before the king and his court at Kew."

He held out his hand, and a woman took it to climb onto the dais. Hair blacker than Quill's swept back from a face with a wide brow and a delicate mouth, as if she thought more than spoke. The fitted crimson velvet of her bodice, edged with gold braid, called attention to her considerable curves.

Applause rang out again.

In the alcove, the quartet that generally accompanied all assembly dances began playing. With a polite smile all around, the professional soprano launched into her repertoire.

"Adieu, adieu my only life.

My duty calls me from thee.

Remember thou'rt a soldier's wife.

Those tears but ill become thee.

What though by duty I am call'd where thund'ring cannons rattle,

Where valor's self might stand appal'd, where valor's self might stand appal'd,

When on the wings of thy dear love to heav'n above thy fervent orifons

Had flown the tender pray'r thou put up there

Shall call a guardian angel down,

Shall call a guardian angel down to watch me in the battle."

He could almost hear the call to arms, smell the gunpowder of the cannon. Moisture dimmed his gaze. He would not wipe at his eyes. Small wonder ancient mariners claimed that the singing of Sirens led sailors to their deaths. He'd have followed that sound.

He managed to keep his composure, and she finished the remaining verses to applause that lasted almost as long as her song. She curtsied, and James hopped back up to join her.

"That is only a taste of Mademoiselle Fortier's abilities. Please stop by the spa at three in the afternoon for the next week, where she will be regaling us. See Mr. Lawrence for subscriptions. This concludes our program for the evening."

The final round of applause waned as attendees rose and began speaking to family and friends. Time to go before anyone attempted closer association. Quill pushed off the wall and turned for the door.

"Captain St. Claire, wait."

He stopped and looked back. Amazing how James could use his magistrate's voice to effect. His friend was shouldering his way through the crowd, the soprano sweeping along beside him.

"Mademoiselle Fortier desired to make your acquaintance," James explained as he and the lady joined Quill. "Mademoiselle, allow me to present Captain Quillan St. Claire."

It wasn't the first time he'd been one of the village's attractions. "Mademoiselle," Quill said with a bow. As he straightened, he glanced to James, who shrugged, though his mouth hinted of a smile. So, his friend saw no underlying reason for the woman to seek Quill, for all she at least pretended a French name.

"Captain," she said with a warm smile, her speaking voice betraying no more of an accent than her singing. She came just under his chin, and her eyes were the color of the sea at dawn, deep blue and not a little mysterious. She knew what to do with those thick, black lashes, for their fluttering beckoned him closer.

"I wanted to thank one of the heroes of the Battle of the Nile," she said. "I have already met many of Lord Nelson's Band of Brothers—Rear Admiral Darby, Rear Admiral Peyton, Captain Berry."

"Then I am indeed in good company," Quill said. "They are excellent commanders. England is fortunate to have them."

"And you as well," she assured him. "I would love to hear more of your exploits. Perhaps we could chat."

That smile implied alone. He had had women make such suggestions in the past. The gilt-frogged uniform of a naval officer tended to turn heads, and never more so than after he'd become known for having fought at one of Britain's greatest naval triumphs over the French.

"You are too kind," he said. "But I fear my wound is encouraging me to decamp this evening."

She made a moue. "So tragic, to be wounded in the service of one's country. Perhaps I could accompany you, provide some comfort."

He shot James another look. His friend was frowning at her, as if he too knew the insistence was far too forward.

"I wouldn't dream of depriving the citizens of Grace-by-the-Sea of your company," Quill said. "And now, I should return you to your adoring audience."

"But of course." She took a step back, then faltered, hand fluttering to her brow. Quill caught her as her knees buckled.

"Mademoiselle?" James asked, taking a step closer. "Are you all right?"

A warm bundle in Quill's arms, she fastened her gaze onto his and refused to look away, even as her fingers dug into his arm. "The performing, it takes a toll."

James stepped back. "I'll fetch our spa physician, Doctor Bennett."

She waved a hand. "No, no. I need no physician. Please, *mon cher capitaine*, would you escort me back to my inn, the Swan?"

Why this insistence on his company? She had to be playing some game beyond a momentary flirtation. The only way to discover the truth of it was to play along.

"Of course," Quill said, setting her gently on her feet. "Did you bring a cloak, a wrap?"

"No," she said, gazing up at him soulfully. "I need only you."

He refused to believe it. "Then we'll be off. James, be so good as to ask Mr. Drummond to assist us."

"Drummond?" she asked, frown gathering, as James strode for the short corridor that led to the door. "I have not been introduced to a Drummond."

"Likely not," Quill explained, leading her toward the door. "He's the local lamplighter. He lost an arm in Flanders. I'm sure you'll want to praise his service as well."

"Of course." Her voice was all flowery sweetness, but, for once, he thought he felt the sting of a bee beneath the words.

Mr. Drummond was waiting as they came out of the assembly rooms. He held his brass lantern high on a pole above his grizzled head to light their way down the street. Some of the other attendees were making their way home, voices soft in the night.

"I have rarely had such a distinguished escort," she told the older man.

Drummond bobbed his head, beard brushing his neckcloth. "The honor is all mine, milady."

"And such a lovely village," she said, glancing at the elegant columns of the spa as they passed it on the right. "I am so glad my schedule allowed me to take part in your musical week. What would you suggest I see while I am here?"

Drummond droned on about the various attractions of the area. She kept her hand on Quill's arm and nodded along, asking a question here, smiling at a quip there. In fact, she gazed at the lamplighter as if he were the most fascinating fellow she'd ever met. She must have them all eating out of the palm of her hand.

Not him.

"And here we are," she sang out as they reached the inn, a two-story rambling structure not far from the spa. "I will not detain you further. Thank you again for seeing me safely back."

"My pleasure," Drummond assured her, beaming. He made no move to leave them.

Mademoiselle Fortier sagged against Quill. "Alas, I find myself overcome by the walk. Perhaps you could see me up to my room, Captain."

She smelled of roses, rich and heady. Her curves brushed his arm. Easy enough to give in, to follow her inside and see if what she offered was as sweet as it seemed.

"I know the owners, the Truants," he said. "I'm sure they can assist you better than I can."

She glanced up at him, and, for one moment, he thought she would call him something vile. Then she seized his lapels, reared up, and pressed her lips against his.

Like silk against his skin, honey on his lips. His hands were coming around her waist before he thought better of it. He was vaguely aware of Drummond leaving them with a chuckle.

In the shadow that dropped as the lantern moved away, she shoved Quill back. "What is wrong with you? I've been trying to get your attention for the last hour. I have a message for you, from Napoleon."

He stared at her, this legend. The pride of His Majesty's Navy, dressed all in black tonight. How the breeze must caress that thick, dark hair as his hooded eyes gazed out at the sea. He had ordered sailors into battle, handed her countrymen one of their most decisive defeats, thwarted Napoleon's plans again and again.

Why was he so dense?

Or was it merely his arrogance that had kept him from taking her lead? She'd certainly faced that before. No one had ever claimed Louis' brother, the Comte d'Artois, was a humble man. Neither were his followers, like her father and his friends. They had all been idealists with no idea of the true cost of things, in time, money, or lives. Why had she thought Quillan St. Claire would be any different?

His hands were still on the waist of her performance gown, fingers tangled in the gold braid. All at once, he pivoted, pulling her around and pinning her against the white-washed wall of the inn. It happened so fast, she lost her breath, she, who had been trained to control it.

"Who are you to speak for Napoleon?" he demanded.

Moonlight sparkled on eyes gone dangerous. Now, that was the legend she had been told to expect.

"One, like you, who wishes to pry out his secrets," she promised him. "I am no pawn of the court. I left Paris with my family during the atrocities. Now I do favors on occasion for the War Office. I was asked to tell you that they have received information about you. The emperor is sending someone to kill you."

He released her and stepped back. "Why should I believe you?"

Marie shrugged, finding breath easier with him a few feet away. "Why not?"

"Because one side of the War Office doesn't speak to the other," he said with disgust. "I have someone I trust there. I don't know you."

"But I know him," she explained. "Markus Dorland,

also formerly of His Majesty's Navy."

He stilled. "Prove that you know Captain Dorland."

She put her hand up next to his ear. "About this tall, sandy hair, vivid blue eyes that can hold you in place with one look."

"Anyone might have noticed that on short acquaintance," he pointed out.

She leaned closer, until she thought for one moment she smelled the sea. "He also was injured at the Battle of the Nile, a blow that took out a chunk of his right calf. He wears padding under his sock to hide the mark."

He crossed his arms over his chest, forcing her to straighten or collide with him anew. "I don't suppose he gave you a letter of introduction."

She tsked. "Certainly not."

He nodded slowly. "Very well. You have delivered your message. You may tell the War Office I will take my usual care."

Which meant none at all. Oh, men!

"That is insufficient," Marie told him. "The information you have been bringing the War Office from France is too important to lose you to chance. I will protect you."

He dropped his arms and laughed.

Laughed.

Anger, humiliation, oh, those were old foes. But this time, she did not try to master them. This time, she used them. With one movement, she yanked out a long hairpin and brought it under his chin. "I know how to protect myself, Captain. I can keep you safe too."

With one movement, he thrust her hand across her body, away from him, and brought himself within inches, holding her in place.

"I can protect myself," he said.

Marie smiled up at him. "You're bleeding. If that pin had been poisoned, you'd be dead shortly."

He released her to step back and touch his neck. As his hand came away, a few drops of blood, black in the moonlight, dotted his glove from the scratch he'd given himself blocking her.

"I've seen enough men die at the tyrant's hand," Marie told him, returning the pin to the coil of her hair. "I won't see another fall because I stood by and did nothing. So, I will cling to you like a tailored coat until we find this Frenchman. Do not try me, Captain. Like you, I do not taste defeat willingly."

Learn more at
www.reginascott.com/sirenscaptain.html.

OTHER BOOKS BY REGINA SCOTT

Marvelous Munroes Series
My True Love Gave to Me
The Rogue Next Door
The Marquis' Kiss
A Match for Mother

Spy Matchmaker Series
The Husband Mission
The June Bride Conspiracy
The Heiress Objective

And other books for Revell, Love Inspired Historical,
and Timeless Regency collections.

ABOUT THE AUTHOR

REGINA SCOTT STARTED WRITING NOVELS in the third grade. Thankfully for literature as we know it, she didn't sell her first novel until she learned a bit more about writing. Since her first book was published, her stories have traveled the globe, with translations in many languages, including Dutch, German, Italian, and Portuguese. She now has had published more than fifty works of warm, witty historical romance.

She loves everything about England, so it was only a matter of time before she started her own village. Where more perfect than the gorgeous Dorset Coast? She can imagine herself sailing along the chalk cliffs, racing her horse across the Downs, dancing at the assembly, and even drinking the spa waters. She drank the waters in Bath, after all!

Regina Scott and her husband of more than 30 years reside in the Puget Sound area of Washington State on the way to Mt. Rainier. She has dressed as a Regency dandy, learned to fence, driven four-in-hand, and sailed on a tall ship, all in the name of research, of course. Learn more about her at her website at www.reginascott.com.

.

CPSIA information can be obtained
at www.ICGtesting.com
Printed in the USA
LVHW021932130521
687357LV00014B/1173